CW00866319

'This charming, tense and gri
number of interesting them
challenges of maturing into an
different faiths; the impact
friendships and parental relationships.

'Interesting to me, as a psychologist and Founder and
Executive Director of 28 Too Many, a charity passionate to
end FGM across Africa and the diaspora, it accurately and
informatively handles this important topic in an educational,
yet sensitive way.

'I highly recommend this book – which moved me to tears
a number of times.'
Dr Ann-Marie Wilson, www.28toomany.org

'This is a very readable, contemporary tale which would
certainly captivate young adults of my acquaintance. As the
story unfolds and the reader is taken through the changing
scenes of a school prom, a road accident, hospital wards, a
Greek island holiday and a people-smuggling incident, there
is an impressive authenticity about the details described. The
underlying activity of a secret agent and the moving account
from a rescued migrant are both arresting and informative.

'Teenage emotions and a growing recognition of the
power of prayer and the relevance of a personal faith are
sensitively introduced into the narrative. There is an honesty
in this, as indeed there is throughout the text, which makes
the book one which I would be happy to recommend widely.'
Jean Howell, former headmistress

THE BELLE OF THE BALL

Is justice, like beauty, ever more than skin deep?

MARY WEEKS MILLARD

instant
ap☐stle

First published in Great Britain in 2017

Instant Apostle
The Barn
1 Watford House Lane
Watford
Herts
WD17 1BJ

British Library Cataloguing-in-Publication Data

A catalogue record for this book is available from the British Library

This book and all other Instant Apostle books are available from Instant Apostle:

Website: www.instantapostle.com
E-mail: info@instantapostle.com

ISBN 978 1 909728 69 1

Printed in Great Britain

Dedication

This book is dedicated to the thousands who have suffered in recent years as migrants trying to cross Europe to find a better life, and to all the young girls who have endured FGM. We pray that soon this barbaric practice will be outlawed in every country of the world.

Acknowledgements

My grateful thanks to Instant Apostle for agreeing to publish this book, and to those who have taken time to read and endorse it.

My grateful thanks to my beloved husband, Malcolm, for all his patience and encouragement while I have been writing it. Your support means so much.

My thanks to my Ugandan 'son', Kabanda, who advised me about the Ugandan part of this story.

My thanks to Lauren and Daniel who pre-read this book for me, commenting on it from a teenager's point of view, and also to Miss Jean Howell, former headmistress of Clarendon School, and Dr Anne-Marie Wilson, founder and president of the charity 28 Too Many, for reading and commending the book.

Chapter one

Lydia was so excited. At last all her school exams had finished. In fact, she was almost finished with school forever – next term she would be at college. Her school uniform could be thrown away – what a relief not to have to wear the much-hated navy blue skirt ever again, or the white blouse and striped tie. She would, of course, keep the blouse she was wearing, because today, everyone in her year group had signed their names on it to celebrate that her exams were finished – and Sam, her date for the prom, had written his name just where her heart was. She'd blushed when he did that, and felt all tingly inside!

Next term, at the sixth form college, she would be allowed to wear whatever clothes she liked – and she was planning to wear her favourite jeans and tops. She would also be allowed to wear dangly earrings and nail polish. At last she would feel that she was really grown up. It was a good feeling and, as she walked home, Lydia put in her earphones and sang along to the latest album she had downloaded onto her smartphone.

Usually Lydia walked home from school with her best friend, Hannah, but today Hannah had stayed behind to practise for a concert that the school orchestra was giving in a couple of weeks' time. Hannah was very musical and played the flute. She was hoping eventually to get a place in a college to study music.

At the zebra crossing over the main road, Lydia took out her earphones – her mum had a 'thing' about being very careful crossing the road. In fact, she had 'things' about many aspects of life. Lydia didn't understand why her mother was always so nervous and safety-conscious, and felt that sometimes she was OTT when it came to carefulness. However, she had promised to do this, and once on the other side she was very close to her grandparents' home. The gate creaked as she opened it and within seconds her grandmother opened the door and welcomed her in.

'How was your day, Dia?' she asked, using her pet name for Lydia. 'Did your last exam go well?'

'I think so, Gran,' she answered. 'It's hard to tell, but I did answer all the questions. I'm so glad that they're all over and now I'm almost finished with school forever!'

'To think my granddaughter will be leaving school!' exclaimed Gran. 'That really makes me feel old. Anyway, come into the kitchen, Dia, I've baked a cake to celebrate the end of the exams. You had better call Gramps, he's out in the garden as usual – you would think our garden was going to be an exhibit at the Chelsea Garden Show, he keeps it so beautiful,' she added, with a twinkle in her eye.

Lydia ran out of the back door and called for her grandfather. He was in the greenhouse, tying up his tomato plants. They chatted together as they went back to the house for the promised cake and tea.

'We've been thinking about you all day,' Gramps said. 'I bet you're glad all those exams are finished. Now you can relax and have some fun with your friends. Have you made any plans for the holidays?'

'Not yet,' answered Lydia. 'I think Mum and Dad have been discussing things – I expect we'll go away at the end of August, as usual.'

As they entered the kitchen, they saw the chocolate cake on the table.

'Oh Gran – you do spoil me!' Lydia said. 'My favourite!'

'Well, you deserve it, love,' commented her gran, as she cut a generous slice for Lydia. 'All these weeks of revision and then exams. I still remember doing my O levels, and feeling glad when they were all over, even if it is a horrible wait until you get the results!'

'Don't remind me, Gran,' answered Lydia, pulling a face, 'but there are good things first, like the prom and then the holidays. Mum told me that you wanted to do a final fitting of my prom dress this afternoon. I'm really excited about wearing it. Did I tell you that Sam Weaver has asked to be my escort? He's so dishy – I can't believe he's asked me. All the girls wanted to be his partner, but he asked me! He hopes to be a footballer for the Crystal Palace team. He's been in the Palace Guards – the junior club – for some years, and they have recruited him for their training academy for next year. That's the only sad thing – he won't be coming to sixth form college with us. Sam is almost six foot already, blond and handsome – with incredible muscles!'

'Your gran will have to get that dress perfect, then, won't she,' laughed Gramps. 'You must be the Belle of the Ball for him! Your gran surely was the Belle of the Ball when she wore it for a Christmas charity ball on our first date. She knocked me for six, I can tell you. I was the luckiest man in the room!'

Hannah was the only person outside the family who had been told about Lydia's choice of dress. All her friends had been talking about their prom dresses for ages, but when she and her mum had gone to London to try to buy a dress which she liked, they just couldn't find anything that looked right on her, certainly not at a price her mum could afford. They had returned home to Croydon tired and fed up, so decided to visit Lydia's grandparents, who lived two roads away from them, and Gran had cheered them up with a cup of tea. It was Gramps who had come up with the idea. He suggested that Lydia try on the ball gown which Gran had worn fifty years before – she still had it wrapped up in black tissue paper and kept in a box under their bed. Lydia didn't want to be rude and say she didn't want an old-fashioned dress – so she had agreed to look at it.

When Gran unwrapped it, Lydia gasped – it was absolutely stunning. The ivory silk still shimmered and the classic style was perfect for her. Gran must have been much slimmer fifty years ago, she thought to herself as she tried on the dress. The ivory colour was fantastic against her olive skin and dark hair – the heritage of her Maltese father. It needed just a little alteration to fit perfectly, and since Gran was a good seamstress, she had promised to do that.

'Now, Henry,' said Gran to her husband. 'Don't go back into the garden. Wait and see Dia when she tries on the dress, and give us your opinion.'

Gramps nodded and picked up the paper while Lydia and her grandmother went upstairs. She tried on the dress. Gran had needed to shorten it just a little, and had used the extra material which she had cut from the hem to make silk roses, one of which she had attached to the bodice. The other she had put on a comb which Lydia could wear in her hair.

Tears came into Gran's eyes when she saw Lydia in the dress – and when she called Henry to come and look, his reaction was the same.

'You look absolutely gorgeous,' he commented, trying to hide the tears in his eyes. Lydia looked at herself in Gran's full-length mirror and had to agree that the dress was fabulous – much nicer than anything she had seen in the shops. The alterations had made it look incredibly modern. She was longing to show Hannah how great it looked. The prom was going to be huge fun, especially with Sam as her escort.

Lydia smiled at her grandparents. She loved them so much and felt so lucky that they lived near and she could spend so much time with them. They were a very special part of her life and she called in almost every day after school. She wanted to continue doing that when she moved on to college in the next school year.

Chapter two

Once the whole year group had finished their exams, the main topic of conversation was the prom. Even the boys were excited, although they tried to pretend they were just going for the sake of the girls, and dancing wasn't really their 'thing'.

It was scheduled to be held in the town's theatre and concert hall, and Lydia, Hannah, their friend Poppy plus their escorts were going to travel to the venue in a white stretch limo. That had come as a complete surprise to them, but Lydia's father, who was away at sea because of his work as the captain of a cruise ship, had arranged it all. She had been amazed when her mum had told her. For many months of the year she saw so very little of her dad that sometimes she almost forgot that he was part of the family. They did visit him on his ship occasionally in the school holidays, or they all went away together to some remote place for a couple of weeks, because he liked to get away from people when he could.

'Life as captain of a cruise ship is a bit like being mayor of a large city, and I like to get away from the noise and bustle when I can,' he had explained to Lydia.

Sometimes he had a few days off and always tried to get home and be with his wife and daughter.

The class of 2016, as the school leavers were called, had decided to arrange their own competition. Everyone attending the prom could have one vote to say who they thought was the Belle of the Ball, and on the last day of term the winner would be announced. This meant that all the girls were talking about their dresses and shoes and how they would have their hair done. Lydia had kept very quiet about her dress. She adored it, but knew her classmates would laugh and ridicule her if they knew that her dress was more than fifty years old and was last worn by her grandmother at a Christmas ball. That just wasn't cool! She wanted to keep it a secret, and Hannah had agreed with her.

Even when Sam asked questions, she just said, 'Wait and see!' He thought she was just being a bit coy. Sam liked girls who were slim and yet had a good figure, and he had decided months before that Lydia was the prettiest girl in their year. He was a bit cocky and quite sure she would say 'yes' when he asked her. He knew he was the best-looking guy in the class and they would be a great couple.

The three girls thought the prom was fantastic. It would be the topic of conversation for days. Lydia thought that it must have been a little like the 'coming out' balls when debutantes were presented to the king or queen in days gone by.

She really felt like a princess that evening. Her mum had arranged for her to have her long, dark, wavy hair straightened and blow-dried, and her nails manicured. Her new shoes were ivory and matched her dress – with just enough heel to give her a little extra height – and she and Hannah had done each other's make-up. They had spent ages finding just the right colour eye shadow and lipstick.

Hannah looked gorgeous, too, in a blue gown that matched the colour of her eyes. Her brothers wolf-whistled when they saw the girls – and they could see the admiration in the eyes of their escorts. Poppy was Irish and always full of fun and jokes. She wore a red gown which matched her personality – always bright and cheerful. They felt very grown up as the limo arrived and the chauffeur opened the doors for them. Sam helped Lydia into the car, and her mother and grandparents waved goodbye as they were driven to the Fairfield Halls.

On arrival, they were greeted by a photographer from the local press, and he took loads of photos; the group of girls and their escorts, single photos, then the class of girls, followed by one of all the boys, and finally, the whole year group. All that took quite a time and the young people were glad when it was over and they could go into the dance.

'Wow!' exclaimed Poppy in amazement. 'Look at all the food in the buffet. To be sure, we'll never eat all that. It's enough to feed the whole school.' Hannah and Lydia agreed. In fact, it looked almost too good to eat, but after a few dances, when people began to feel hungry, the plates of food soon began to disappear.

The band was lively and played songs that were well known. Even those who were shy began to relax and enjoy themselves.

The evening passed in a happy daze. It was huge fun, except when one of the boys in her tutor group whom Lydia didn't really like tried to steal a kiss. However, Sam saw him and soon put a stop to that. Lydia was his girl for that evening (and she hoped it would stay that way). Sam looked so handsome, and she was proud to be with him and dance with him. When he held her close she felt her body reacting in a way which was exciting, but also a little scary. She wondered if Poppy and Hannah felt the same when they were dancing with their dates. She glanced around the room and saw Hannah being whirled around by Joe, and could see she was having fun.

At the end of the prom, the three girls and their partners found the limo waiting for them, and one by one they were dropped at their homes. Hannah and Poppy had been taken home, and then, as they reached Lydia's house, Sam kissed her before he helped her out of the limo and walked her up the path. Somehow the feel of his lips on hers made her sure that he was now her boyfriend.

Lydia opened the door quietly, still revelling in the feel of Sam's lips on her own. She found her mum was waiting up for her.

'Tell me all about it,' she said. 'Was it great fun?'

Once she started talking, Lydia just couldn't stop describing the dancing, the food, the lovely dresses the girls were wearing, and how they had played many of her favourite songs. It was ages before they went to bed, but eventually her mother insisted they get some sleep because she had to work the next day. She worked as a sister on the children's ward at the local hospital, and that meant long shifts. That was one reason why Lydia spent so much time with her grandparents, so that she wasn't alone at home if her mum was on a late or a night shift.

Before she locked up the house for the night, her mother had a strange routine where she looked at lights and under beds and checked everywhere about six times. Lydia really couldn't understand her mum's obsessions, but had stopped asking questions years ago, as she had never received any satisfactory answers. She just accepted that that was the way her mum was.

As they went upstairs to bed, Lydia asked her mother about the summer holidays. 'Will we be going away this year? Are we joining Dad on his ship or will he holiday with us somewhere else?'

'Dad was thinking of meeting us somewhere in the Highlands of Scotland – he wants to get away from people and just be with us. You know he finds living on a floating city most of the time too noisy and crowded. He'll probably Skype us in a day or so. I have booked the last two weeks of August as holiday anyway.'

'Good, that sounds cool,' answered Lydia. 'I wish we saw him more often – sometimes I don't feel like I really have a dad – although of course I do, and I do love him.'

'I know, dear, but being the captain of the ship means he doesn't get away very often and he also has extra journalistic work on top of that. Even I don't understand all of that, but it means he needs be very careful of what he says, even a bit secretive. We must just accept and understand that is the way it is, but he does love us both very much. That's what really matters,' answered her mum, giving her a hug and a kiss.

When she was in bed, Lydia kept thinking about her father. If only he had been around to see her this evening in her lovely dress – why couldn't he Skype or even just phone her every day? How could his job as the captain of a cruise ship have a secretive side? The questions kept filling her mind and it was a long time before she dropped off to sleep.

Chapter three

The last few days of term just flew past. Lydia felt both happy and sad.

'How can you feel both happy and sad at the same time?' she asked Hannah.

Her friend laughed and answered, 'I don't know, but I understand just what you mean. I feel the same. I'm happy all the exams are over, that we're leaving school and going on to the next stage of our lives, but sad to say goodbye to some of our friends who are not coming to sixth form college with us, as well as some of the teachers who have been great. It's a weird feeling!'

At their last assembly, the result of the ballot taken after the prom was read out. The headmaster read it as if it were in a reality show and the results really mattered.

'The Belle of the Ball is …' A long silence ensued, and all the girls waited nervously. '… Lydia Rocco!'

Everyone clapped and cheered and Lydia went very pink. What would Gran think? She couldn't wait to tell her and her mum. Afterwards her friends hugged and congratulated her. Her escort, Sam, put his arm around her and kissed her cheek in front of everyone. That caused even greater uproar!

'Can I take you on a date – maybe to see a film and then for a meal?' he asked.

'Oh, yes please, Sam, I'd love that,' Lydia answered, thinking to herself that it would be her first real date and perhaps the start of a special friendship.

Hannah and Lydia gathered their belongings and, after many 'goodbyes' and making sure they had everybody's phone numbers and email addresses, they started to walk home together. As they went, Lydia sent a text to her mother, who was at work, to tell her about the vote, and told her she would call in and tell her grandparents the news since they didn't 'do' texting and really hated mobile phones and other modern technology.

The girls reached the zebra crossing and Lydia said goodbye to Hannah who didn't cross the main road. They arranged to meet up the next morning and browse around in the shopping mall. When the lights changed, Lydia started to walk over the road. Suddenly she saw a streak of silver coming at her. It was as if everything within her froze. The next thing she knew was that she was lying on the ground and her body was in terrible pain. She thought she heard someone call her name before everything went black. It was to be a very long time before she woke up.

Hannah had seen it happen – all at lightning speed. A silver car had appeared as if from nowhere, hit Lydia almost as if it was intended, and then sped off without stopping. The picture was impressed on her mind; she was sure that she would never forget the scene – or seeing Lydia in a crumpled heap in the road. At first, she felt paralysed by the shock, but then ran over to Lydia and called her name. There was no response. Quickly she dialled 999 on her phone. By then other people were coming to help. Hannah wasn't 'into' praying to God, as her parents were, but she called out to Him now from the bottom of her heart, begging Him to send help and save Lydia's life.

It seemed like hours as she waited, kneeling by her best friend, sobbing and praying – but in fact it was only minutes before the police and ambulance arrived. A policewoman led her away and gently asked what had happened. Hannah tried to explain who Lydia was and where her mother worked, where her grandparents lived and how the silver car had appeared from nowhere, gone through the red light, hit Lydia and raced off at speed.

'I'm going to take you home as soon as we have informed Lydia's mother, but tomorrow I will have to come back and ask you all the questions again, so that you can make a statement. Can you just stay in the squad car for a few minutes?' the policewoman asked kindly. Hannah nodded. She closed her eyes – she didn't want to look at the paramedics who were trying to save Lydia's life. She felt her heart was bursting with pain – if only they had talked for five more minutes, maybe her friend would not have been hit. If only… If only… Those two words reverberated around and around in her head.

Suddenly there was a loud whirring noise and Hannah opened her eyes and saw the air ambulance landing on the road and the doctors running towards Lydia. She knew that things must be very, very bad for her to be airlifted to hospital.

In time the policewoman returned and spoke to Hannah. 'Things are looking very bad for your friend. She is being flown to Atkinson Morley Hospital. They can give her the best treatment for her head injuries. Now, let me drive you home. Is your mother in?'

'She should be, and so should my brothers. This was my last day at school, so Mum promised to be home from work early,' sobbed Hannah, giving her address to the police officer.

Chapter four

A policewoman had collected Lydia's mother, Jane, from the Croydon University Hospital where she worked and driven her to Atkinson Morley Hospital. Even with flashing lights, the journey seemed to Jane to take forever. It was rush hour and the streets were clogged with cars and buses, and they found it hard to make room for the police car to get past them. Jane sat in the front of the car, a soggy tissue in her hand, trying not to keep on crying in spite of the huge lump in her throat. She felt so scared and so alone. The policewoman was kind enough, but wasn't able to talk much to Jane as she had to concentrate on driving through the heavy traffic.

When they arrived at the hospital, Jane was ushered into the Accident and Emergency department. Fortunately, being a nurse by profession, she was used to hospitals and all the equipment and personnel in such a busy department, but even so, she felt lost and unsure of herself. The police officer took care of all the details and soon she was taken to a room where Lydia was being treated. Jane thanked the policewoman for all her help and sat down on a chair, totally in shock. Every minute seemed like an hour. Would her daughter recover? If she did, would she be 'normal' or would there be long-term brain damage? The clock in the room seemed to be ticking very loudly, but Jane could still hear the medical staff talking softly as they worked together.

'Her blood pressure is dropping,' someone said. Jane's heart went cold. Was Lydia dying? Although not a church attender, she began to pray, with tears streaming down her face.

'Oh, God,' she whispered in her heart. 'If you are real, please help my Lydia. Please let her live.'

A young nurse, wearing green scrubs, came and sat beside her. She took Jane's hand and spoke to her.

'Mrs Rocco,' she said gently, 'we are doing all we can for your daughter. She is very badly injured and we are trying to stabilise her condition. As soon as this happens she will go to theatre for surgery to release the pressure on her brain and to try to tie off the blood vessels which are bleeding. She has multiple fractures, too, but for now, these will just be splinted. We need to get the bleeding in her brain to stop. The broken bones will be set later. After the surgery, she will be taken into the Intensive Care Unit, where they have a bed ready for her. Once she is there and settled, I'll come and get you and you can sit with her. We will make a bed beside her for you, too.

'Now, can I take you to the office and we can have a cup of tea and you can ask me the questions which must be running through your mind – and I can ask you for your daughter's details?'

Jane nodded. How often she had been the kind nurse who had taken a shocked and worried parent into her office? Now it was her turn, and she almost didn't know what to ask; or maybe just didn't dare to ask.

The cup of tea did help to calm her down and she gave all the information to the nurse and began to ask a few questions. Jane also realised that she needed to contact her husband, and that wasn't always quite as simple as it might seem. Her mind was in overdrive wondering if her daughter's accident was just that – a terrible, but unfortunate accident; or could it be something more sinister, something she had always dreaded might happen to her family? Could she trust this nurse? Could she even trust the police? Could she trust anybody any more? She had lived with her fears for so long now – fears that she and Lydia might be attacked because she knew her husband was investigating situations of injustice in the world. Yes, he was the captain of a cruise ship, and loved his work, but he had always had such a burning desire to right some of the wrongs in the world that he couldn't help but get involved in situations which put them into danger. Jane also knew that of late she had become almost paranoid, living on her nerves, worrying about safety all the time.

The nurse's bleep sounded and Jane was left with her own thoughts for a few minutes. Once again, she silently cried out to God for help – not just for Lydia, but how and when to contact her husband, John. Jane suddenly knew she must contact her parents, too. Lydia should have gone to them after school and they would be sick with worry because she hadn't turned up. As soon as the nurse returned, Jane asked if it was OK to use her mobile and phone her parents – explaining that Lydia would have been on her way there when she was knocked down.

'Of course you can, Mrs Rocco. Also please feel free to use the office phone if you prefer. I'll wait outside while you do that. Maybe you also would like to ask someone to be with you for a while. The bleep was to tell me that Lydia was stabilised and has just gone into theatre. It may be some hours before she gets to ICU. It is good news that she was stabilised so quickly.'

'Thank you,' answered Jane. 'I need to phone my parents. I'm a sister on the children's ward at the Croydon University Hospital in Thornton Heath, so I need to inform them that I won't be at work for the time being; my husband is the captain of a cruise liner and it might take me a while to contact him.'

Lydia's grandmother answered the phone and Jane tried very hard to make the situation sound less serious than it actually was, as she told her mother what had happened.

'Dia is stable and is having an operation to stop the bleeding in her brain. When she is stable enough, her broken bones will need to be set. For now, they will be immobilised in splints. I will stay here to be with her when she wakes up. I'll keep you informed about her progress, but try not to worry too much,' she told them. She was good at being calm and reassuring with the relatives of her own patients – and managed to be so now, even though her insides were in turmoil.

Jane then spoke to her own nursing officer and was told not to worry about work until Lydia was out of danger, and she also phoned Hannah because she knew that she would be very worried. Hannah's mum answered and promised to send her daughter round to Lydia's grandparents the next day to make sure they were coping with the situation.

'What about you, Jane?' Hannah's mother, Pauline, asked her, 'Can I come over and keep you company for a while? I'll get my church friends to pray for Lydia, too, if you would like that,' she added.

'Yes, please, to both,' answered Jane. 'And thank you so much. Lydia's very badly injured and I don't know if she'll get through this. I can't think straight.'

Chapter five

Those first few hours of waiting at the hospital were torment for Lydia's mother. Her nurses' training was of little help to her because she knew only too well what the outcome could be from such severe head trauma. She was very glad when Pauline arrived. They had been friends ever since their two girls had started at pre-school together.

'I can stay with you all night,' Pauline told her friend. 'Mark has come home from work and is with the children, and one of my friends will come after breakfast and stay until I get home. You shouldn't be on your own at a time like this.'

'Thank you so much,' replied Jane. 'Just having someone to talk to makes such a difference. I'm still waiting to get a direct line to John. He has extra work which can take him off the ship and then it isn't so easy to contact him. His mobile seems to be switched off – isn't that always the case when you need someone urgently? If you don't mind, I'll use the sister's phone and contact someone here in the London office who is usually able to get hold of John in an emergency for me.'

'Of course I don't mind. I'll sit and pray you get through quickly. John needs to get here as soon as he can,' replied Pauline. She gave Jane a big hug as she went to phone.

Jane shut the door of the sister's office. She knew she had to get hold of her husband because Lydia was so critically ill, but she still had to be a bit discreet about it. Trying not to cry, Jane punched in her husband's mobile number again – it was still switched off. Then she phoned the ship and spoke to the first mate and explained what had happened to Lydia. He was very concerned and told her that her husband was on shore and off duty, but they would keep trying to contact him. With this information, she phoned the London number she had been given and was thankful when it was answered straight away. The person on the phone knew exactly where John was and what he was doing, and promised to get hold of him very quickly. Jane explained her fears that it might not have just been a hit-and-run accident but something more sinister.

'Thank you, Mrs Rocco,' he answered. 'I promise I will get your husband home as soon as possible. We'll arrange a flight to London as soon as we can. He should phone you within the next half-hour. I understand your fears, and be assured, we will investigate the accident thoroughly. I hope your daughter will soon recover.'

Jane felt relieved and went back to Pauline.

'John will be flown home as soon as possible – and he should phone me in the next half an hour. Let's hope that Lydia will make it through the surgery.'

'Why don't we have a break and go to the hospital restaurant?' suggested Pauline. 'You can use your mobile there when John rings. I'll tell the nurse where we're going – I expect Lydia will be a few more hours in the theatre. Surgery takes a long time.'

As they walked through the long hospital corridors, Jane began to feel sick. The smell of disinfectant, which she had been so used to all her working life, suddenly seemed to reach her throat and threaten to choke her. She grabbed Pauline's arm, and was so glad when they arrived at the restaurant and she could sit down. They found a table in a corner, well away from the staff who were coming for their evening meals. Her phone began to vibrate in her pocket, and Jane was thankful to see it was John's number. Pauline left her to talk privately to him and went to the counter to order drinks and something to eat. She knew Jane probably wouldn't feel like eating, but it was important for them to have some sustenance for the long night ahead.

Through her tears, Jane told John what had happened, and he reassured her that he would be with her the next morning – the flight had been arranged and a car was ordered to get him to the nearest airport.

'Hang on in there, darling,' John encouraged her. 'Lydia will need us both to be strong and help her through this. I'm glad Pauline is with you – thank her from me. I need to get back to the ship and grab a few things and head out to the airport. I'll soon be with you – love you both so much – tell that to Lydia. Bye.'

When Pauline arrived with the tray, Jane had wiped her tears and felt more in control. John was on his way home and somehow, because of that, she felt sure that Lydia would make it through the night. She managed a weak smile for Pauline and gratefully drank the tea and even nibbled a little food.

A few hours later, they were informed that Lydia had survived the surgery and was now in recovery. Shortly after that they were taken to the ICU where Lydia was now being treated. Jane was glad that she was a nurse and at least understood what all the monitors and tubes were for, but her daughter looked very frail and had many severe injuries. Jane could see that her daughter's beautiful face was severely scarred, and it saddened her, even though she knew that facial scarring wasn't life-threatening.

'Lydia is stable now,' the consultant informed them. 'We have put her into an induced coma, and expect that it will be several days, if not weeks, before we can allow her to wake up. We need her brain to rest and the swelling to decrease. Her broken bones will mend in time and I am thankful to say that it appears she has no spinal injuries. She is a young and healthy girl, so has a good chance of making it through this.'

'Thank you, thank you for all you have done for my daughter,' Jane said to the consultant as he left the cubicle. Pauline and Jane looked at each other and hugged.

'Thank you, Lord,' Pauline whispered, and Jane nodded.

It was, indeed, several weeks before the drugs were reduced and Lydia was allowed to come out of the coma. Lydia's dad had arrived back in England the day after the accident, and he and her mum kept a constant vigil at her bedside day and night. They had lots of time to talk together and to think of the future.

'As soon as my present assignment is complete, I'm going to ask for sabbatical leave,' John told his wife. 'We need time together as a family. In fact, maybe I should get a shore-based job from now on.'

'It would be so lovely to be a "normal" family again, but you must do what you think best, John. You have the sea in your blood and I'm not sure you would be happy in a land-based job,' answered Jane.

'That's so true,' answered John. 'Sitting here with you both has given me time to think. Often my mind goes back to my childhood days in Malta. My mother called me John because she wanted me to grow up to be like a knight of the Order of St John. It appealed to me so much, to be like a knight in shining armour, and I dreamed of helping others, especially to stand up for justice for the underdogs of our society. I was a dreamy-eyed youngster. Child though I was, I went many times into the cathedral of St John in Valletta. It is so beautiful – I'm sure you remember me taking you there. I used to sit quietly, just awestruck at the magnificence of it.

'I remember gazing up at the enormous Caravaggio painting of the beheading of St John the Baptist. It made me so angry that he had been killed to satisfy the whim of Herod's wife – I vowed then I would try my best to help the weak and the poor. That's what drives me to do the extra work as well as captaining the ship. It's never been about the money, and I always hoped that it would never endanger you or Lydia. I feel so guilty now.'

'We don't know that it was an intentional attack on her, John,' replied Jane. 'The police haven't caught the culprit yet. It won't help any of us if you blame yourself.'

'I know, but there is always the "if only" that reverberates around my head,' answered John. 'When she wakes up and is better, I want to explain to her more why I feel so strongly about helping people who are unable to help themselves. We'll go back to Malta and I'll show her the painting. I'll take her to Valletta harbour and we'll sit and look at the boats together. My brothers and I spent hours at the harbour – it's where I grew to love the sea and sea-faring. I'll take her, too, to the exhibition of the Knights Hospitallers in the Holy Infirmary – you remember it, the *Sacra Infermeria*. Parts of the building go back to 1574. We'll spend so much more time together and I'll teach her about her Maltese heritage. We'll wander together around the Grand Harbour.'

'Lydia will love that – and she has said sometimes that she misses having her dad around. Time spent with you and learning about your roots will be really special for her. I just hope that when she wakes up her brain will not be damaged. I guess that it my great fear,' admitted Jane.

'Mine, too,' said John. He reached out for his wife's hand and squeezed it. 'We must hope and pray for the best.'

Chapter six

Hannah came regularly to visit Lydia. At first, she was horrified to see all the wires, monitors and the state of Lydia's limbs, which were by now in plaster casts, but she soon became used to all these things. Even though Lydia was unconscious, Hannah told her all about the things she and her brothers were doing in the holidays, and how she was putting updates about Lydia's condition every day on Facebook and about all the answers from their friends, because the nurses had said that Lydia could hear what she said.

'Sam says "get well soon", and he is looking forward to his date with you when you are better,' Hannah told her. 'Maybe we'll have a double date as I'm seeing Joe. He's good company. I don't think I have any real feelings for him, though. Maybe they will come in time. I miss doing things with you so much.'

Lydia's parents had been warned that she could have permanent brain damage, but no one would know until she came out of her coma. Everyone was very anxious when the drugs were decreased, gradually allowing Lydia to wake up. The process took about three days and Hannah was visiting when Lydia's eyelids flickered and opened. She pressed the bell for the nurse, who came rushing in.

'Please get Lydia's mum and dad – they're in the café,' she told the nurse. 'Lydia's opened her eyes!'

Everyone was back by her bed within seconds, just in time to hear Lydia say in a tiny voice, 'Where am I?' It was the most wonderful question ever asked, because it meant that Lydia could think and speak and see. Hannah couldn't wait to get home and post the news on Facebook – and on the bus going back to Croydon she remembered to thank God for answering all their prayers.

Once Lydia was out of the coma, her recovery continued well. She had lots of the tubes and monitors removed so that she could be taken to an ordinary ward. The physiotherapists helped her to sit up, then gradually she was able get up and into a chair by her bed.

As soon as she was fit enough, Lydia had to be interviewed by the police. She struggled to remember and put together what had happened on the afternoon of the accident. All she could see in her mind's eye was a streak of silver coming towards her as she crossed the road – then pain and blackness. She told the policeman this – but the more she tried to remember, the worse her headache became.

One afternoon Sam came to visit her. He was training hard with the youth team of Crystal Palace, and had been signed on as an apprentice. Sam had thought for a long time of what he could take for Lydia – flowers were no longer allowed in hospitals, and somehow grapes or chocolates didn't seem quite right, so in the end he had bought her a Crystal Palace top and shorts, which she could wear as pyjamas while she was in hospital.

That afternoon, when he walked through the ward door, Lydia looked up and saw the boy who had been her escort to the prom. She remembered the dress; she remembered being chosen as the Belle of the Ball and her excitement going home and how much she had wanted to share the news with Gran and Gramps. She smiled. Sam looked as gorgeous as ever, and had promised her a date – her first grown-up date! Her insides fluttered as she remembered their kiss after the prom and then, again, on the last day of term.

Sam looked at Lydia and tried to smile. Where was the dark-haired beauty he had known? Her hair was stubby and short where it had been shaved before the operation; she was thin and pale with dark shadows under her eyes. She had some bad scars on her face – he felt repulsed. This couldn't be the girl he had hoped would be his girlfriend! Something of revulsion flickered over his face, even though he tried to control it. Hannah had warned him that Lydia had changed because of all she had gone through, but he never thought she would look as she did! Her legs and arms were still in plaster and it occurred to him that she might even end up in a wheelchair. She was not the gorgeous girl he had known at school – he didn't want her as his girl.

Embarrassed, Sam handed her the gift. 'I thought you might like to support me, but I have to rush away for a training practice. I hope you get better soon. Sorry I can't stay longer,' he said, and quickly left the ward.

Lydia's mum was also visiting. She saw her daughter's face and the disappointment spreading over it.

'Never mind, love,' she said in a comforting voice. 'Some people, especially men, just can't hack hospitals. They hate the smell and even sometimes faint. I've seen it happen so many times. Maybe he'll come and visit when you get home.'

'Maybe,' answered Lydia, but deep down inside she knew that she wouldn't see Sam again. He would look for someone else. She might never again look as she did when she was Belle of the Ball, even after her scars healed. She undid the parcel and gazed at the Palace kit – she would never wear the top and shorts. Her mother put them away in the locker, sad for her daughter, but in a way glad that she hadn't become deeply involved with a boy who thought more about what she looked like on the outside than who she was on the inside, but knowing, too, that the rejection was so hurtful for her. Lydia had come through so much, but still had to come to terms with the fact that she might be physically scarred for life – a terrible thing for any teenager to face.

Not long after that, Hannah woke one morning with that awful feeling of 'butterflies' in her stomach. It was a Thursday – the longed-for yet dreaded Thursday in the middle of August when the GCSE results were due. Her mother had promised to drive her to school that morning to get her results, but somehow, whatever they were, it wouldn't be the same without Lydia being there. They had always shared everything, as best mates do, the good and the bad.

When she arrived at school she found that a lot of her classmates were already there, some whooping with delight, but others obviously disappointed and wanting to be on their own. Hannah was given her envelope by the school secretary – and then she hesitated.

'What about Lydia Rocco's results?' she asked. 'I'll be going to the hospital this afternoon.'

'I'm afraid that I can't allow you to take them,' the secretary told her, shaking her head sadly. 'It's against the rules. But I will phone her parents and remind them that they are here and I expect one of them will collect them. How is she getting on, Hannah? When I heard about the accident I was so sad – such a lovely girl!'

'She's getting better slowly,' answered Hannah. 'It's going to take a long time, but it was wonderful on the day she woke up – we all knew then that there was hope for her.'

Hannah thanked the secretary and moved out of the way as others from her year group were arriving for their results. She looked at the envelope and felt sick. In one way the results of the exams were important, but in another, what did it really matter compared to being strong and well? Lydia might have all As or A*s – but what good would that be if her brain didn't recover properly?

Hannah decided to go to the toilets and open her envelope, where no one else could see her. As she opened it, her hands shook. Her eyes were blurred as she tried to read, and even when she saw her grades were better than she had hoped for, her happiness was dimmed as she thought of Lydia.

When Hannah felt calm enough, she went back to the school hall and faced her classmates who wanted to know her grades. 'I've got better than I thought,' she answered, 'and all I need for the sixth form college – but I must run, my mum is waiting for me.'

Hannah's mum had parked in a quiet road nearby – she seemed to understand how her daughter felt. They looked at the results together and her mum hugged her and told her how very proud she was.

'We must phone Dad,' she said. 'Everyone in the office will want to know!' That made Hannah laugh, for several of the people with whom her dad worked were always asking him about his family. She phoned him at once, and was thrilled to hear how pleased he was. Then she phoned Lydia's mother, reminding her to collect Lydia's results, just in case the secretary was too busy or forgot to phone her.

Hannah by this time was used to catching the buses she needed to get to Atkinson Morley Hospital, and she tried to visit Lydia most days. They sat and looked at a magazine, chatted a little, and occasionally watched a bit of a DVD. Lydia struggled to concentrate and often had bad headaches. Sometimes she was very frustrated at the slowness of her recovery, although the medical staff all seemed to think she was a living miracle and doing very well.

That Thursday afternoon when Hannah arrived, she found her friend excited.

'I'm doing so well that the consultant has said that I can be transferred to the Croydon University Hospital for rehabilitation. As soon as there is a bed, I'll be moved! It'll be so much easier for Mum, and also Gran and Gramps will be able to come more often, and you won't have those long bus journeys.'

'P'raps Sam will come and see you – it's not far from the Crystal Palace grounds,' commented Hannah. 'You had better get out your kit to wear as pyjamas!'

'I don't think he will,' Lydia answered, sadly. 'I saw his face when he came that time – it was as if I disgusted him. He wanted the Belle of the Ball for his girlfriend, and not someone who will be disfigured for life, like me.' A couple of tears sprang into her eyes, and she quickly wiped them away. 'Even I can't bear to look at myself in the mirror. The scars might fade a bit, but we all know that this huge one will never go away,' she continued, drawing her finger down a long scar from her forehead to her chin.

'Then he's not worth bothering about, Lyd,' Hannah said quickly. 'Your scars will heal and look much less noticeable than now, and anyway, my mum has always told me that beauty comes from the inside; it's about character and not good looks! Do you remember how chubby I was at primary school? I used to get teased and bullied a lot, and although I tried to laugh it off, it hurt so much inside. You were always my friend and stuck up for me – you were always beautiful inside, and that's the real you.'

Just then the ward door opened and in walked Lydia's parents.

'Hi, sweetie,' they said, bending to kiss their daughter. 'Hi, Hannah – congratulations!'

'Congratulations? What for?' asked Lydia.

'It's exam results day – and I passed well, except for Geography, I only got an E in that,' Hannah answered.

'Oh! I had forgotten all about them,' replied Lydia. 'Did I do well?'

'You had better look and see,' answered her dad, handing over the envelope. 'We collected it from school before we came, that's why we're a bit late.'

Lydia took the envelope and tore it open. Her eyes took a while to focus, for she still had problems with that.

'The writing is a bit too small, can you read them for me, Han?' she asked. Hannah looked at Lydia's parents who nodded in assent.

'Wow! You've done brilliantly,' she said. 'A* in French and German; A in both English exams; B for Maths, History, Science and Art; C for Geography – I knew you'd beat me at that! – and D for Technical Drawing.'

'Have I really, that's amazing! I must get better quickly so that we can be at college together,' Lydia answered, brightly.

All the excitement had made Lydia very tired, and suddenly her eyes were doing very funny things and her whole body began to shake. She didn't know what was happening. Hannah was nearest to the bell and rang for the nurse, while her parents drew the curtains around the bed and then ran for help. Hannah felt very scared because her friend wasn't 'with it' and couldn't speak to her. She was so relieved when the medical staff arrived to deal with the situation.

'Lydia has had an epileptic fit,' explained the doctor, once everything was back in control and she was asleep. 'The excitement must have triggered it. I'm afraid that this might well be an ongoing problem for her, and because of her severe head injuries she could be liable to have a seizure at any time. We will give her medication to control the fits, but it might take a while for us to find the right dose for her. The good news is that I still think she can be transferred to your local hospital this weekend – she really is making a remarkable recovery.'

Hannah was rather subdued as Lydia's parents drove her home after their daughter had been settled down to sleep. Would Lydia really be able to return to a normal life? She prayed fervently in her mind that she would, and that the man who drove that silver car would be found and punished.

As she got out of the car, Lydia's father tried to comfort Hannah, because he could see how upset she was.

'This is still a day of celebration, Hannah. You have both done so well in your exams. Lydia is coming nearer home and I promise you, as soon as she is well enough, we will have a holiday and if you are allowed, you will come with us and have some fun. We couldn't wish for Lydia to have a better friend and you are like another daughter to us!'

'Thank you,' Hannah said quietly, then ran up her drive. The front door was opened by her brothers, who shouted 'surprise', and she was ushered in to find a big family party waiting for her to celebrate her success!

Chapter seven

Towards the end of August, Lydia had been discharged from the hospital. She was very weak, both her legs were still in plaster and one of them had metal screws poking through to hold the bones in the right position, but she was very determined to do all the exercises she had been taught, so that she would get strong again. She still hated to look in a mirror as the scars on her face were so disfiguring – but until her hair grew again she had a wig to wear. The wig was made of long, dark hair, as her own had been, and the fringe covered her face a bit, so she put up with the fact that it was hot weather, which made it feel itchy to wear, because she knew she looked more 'normal'.

Her dad had returned to his ship, but with the promise that they would all have a holiday on one of the Greek Islands in early September, and this gave Lydia a target to aim for. She would make sure she was fit enough to enjoy the holiday. Her father had also given serious thought about a change of career, and informed the shipping line and his other employer of his intentions. He could not endanger his family again, for in his mind, he was sure that Lydia's accident was somehow connected with the investigatory work with which he was involved.

Lydia's mum, too, had been able to return to work once her daughter had been transferred to the same hospital in Croydon, but after she was discharged her grandparents spent a lot of time with her, so that she would not be left on her own. This was one of the directions which the medical staff at the hospital had insisted upon. They had informed the family that a fit could happen without warning, at any time, and so at this stage of recovery Lydia should not be left alone. To begin with she was very cross about this, for it made her feel that she was being treated like a child, but as the days went by she was secretly glad to have someone near all the time. In fact, she was very scared of going outside the house. The fit had been such a frightening experience and for several days afterwards she had felt very strange. She had been told that her brain still needed time to recover fully from the trauma of the accident and surgery, and the drugs would need adjusting regularly through this period.

Just before the holiday, something happened which caused Lydia and her mother to become very scared, once again. An anonymous letter had been posted through their front door.

Jane was at home when she heard something drop through the letterbox. As she opened the envelope and read the message, her hands began to shake and she felt sick. Reaching the lounge, she sank into the nearest chair and all the colour drained from her face.

'Mum,' said Lydia, in alarm. 'Whatever's the matter? You look as if you've seen a ghost. Whatever does that letter say?'

'It's nothing, darling,' Jane tried to say, but tears began to appear in her eyes and she started to shake with fear. Lydia knew there must be really bad news in the letter, and lifted herself out of her chair, grabbed her crutches and hobbled over to her mother. She took the letter from her hand and looked at it.

The words had been cut out of a newspaper and stuck onto a piece of writing paper. It read:

SO YOU SURVIVED. THAT WAS NOT PART OF THE
PLAN. NEXT TIME YOU WILL NOT BE SO LUCKY.
YOU WILL PAY FOR YOUR FATHER'S SINS.

Lydia almost fell as she read, then reread the message. No wonder her mother was upset. For a moment, Lydia thought she was going to fall, her knees went so weak. She began to shake and a great wave of fear came over her that she was going to have another fit. She somehow hobbled back to her chair, the piece of paper still in her hand.

'Do you think this is a real threat?' she asked her mum, 'or could it be a sick joke?'

'I don't know, Lydia, but we have to treat it as real. We need to take it seriously. There are some evil and sick people out there who care nothing about anybody else and will do anything to promote their own cause. Let's see if we can get hold of your dad and ask his advice. I guess it will be a police matter,' Jane replied.

'Dad did explain to me that he was doing some investigative journalism into people smuggling. He told me about his name and how it linked with the Knights of St John in Malta. Somehow, I understand now why he feels it important to investigate and expose things which are unjust in our world. I am proud of him. I think we should Skype him right away, then phone the police.'

Lydia's mother's hands were still shaking badly as she called her husband on her smartphone. He answered at once – she could see that he was at dinner and other people were around him.

'I'm sorry to disturb you, John, but can you excuse yourself and talk privately. We have a big problem here,' she explained.

Within minutes John was in his private cabin and he could see how upset both Jane and Lydia were. His first reaction to the letter was anger. If only he could get his hands on the person who tried to murder his daughter and was now threatening to do so again!

'This is a police matter, Jane. Lock all the doors and phone the police at once,' he told her in a tight voice. 'I will also phone my contacts and let them know what's going on. The sooner I get you all away from there, the better.'

The next phone call was to the local police, who responded very quickly. They were still trying to find out who had been the hit-and-run driver, but so far there had been no clues. Maybe this letter would now lead to their arrest. It was utterly terrifying both to the family and to the police to think that something even worse than the accident might happen to Lydia. They took the threat very seriously.

One of the first things the police did was to help Jane get new locks and bolts fitted on all the doors and make sure the property was as secure as it possibly could be. They discussed putting Jane and Lydia into a 'safe house', but as their holiday was imminent it was decided that a policewoman would be assigned to look after them. Her name was Constable Stevens, and she would live in with them, patrol the area and try to ensure their safety. When she was off duty, another policewoman would take her place. This meant that Jane would be able to go to work and know that Lydia was safe. Lydia's grandparents had to be told about the threat, but they still came each day to spend time with Lydia.

It was a relief when the day arrived for them to go on holiday. Lydia was scared to walk outside, scared to go in a car for her hospital appointments and scared about the flight they would have, and her mother had become doubly diligent in checking everywhere to ensure they were safe. They had been promised a police escort to the airport and would be guarded until they were safely on the plane. In fact, they didn't know exactly where they were going; it had all been arranged by John – that bit was quite exciting, if scary!

Fortunately, everything went to plan, and on a sunny morning Lydia, her mother and Hannah set off in a chauffeur-driven car to an RAF base, from where they were flown out to Samos.

'Who would have thought that we would have all this special treatment?' remarked Lydia as they boarded the plane. She had been wheeled out in her wheelchair and then lifted by two good-looking young airmen into the plane.

'I wish I had my legs in plaster, too!' said Hannah, with a laugh. 'I'd like to be carried by two dishy airmen!'

Once they were safely on board, everyone sighed with relief and began to relax. They'd had no idea that they would be going on a special flight. Hannah was already thinking about the story she would be able to share on social media after the holiday. She knew that for now it had to be secret because everything was about keeping Lydia safe. She knew her brothers would be green with envy at her adventure when they were eventually allowed to hear the story.

John was waiting for them at the little airport in Samos. As Jane and Hannah stepped down and then Lydia was carried from the plane, it was wonderful to feel the sunshine and warmth, having left a damp, drizzly London. It wasn't *too* hot, but the weather was just perfect for a holiday. After hugs and kisses all round, they drove to the hotel where they were to stay. It was situated a little way around the coast – not in a town or even a village, but right on the seafront. The sky was clear blue, as was the sea. There was a fine pebble beach and tamarisk trees on the promenade, blowing in the gentle breeze. It seemed idyllic, and as she looked around, Jane hoped and prayed that they could put the nightmare of the past few months behind them.

When they entered the hotel, they were warmly welcomed and then shown to their rooms. Lydia's parents had one room, and right next to it the girls shared another. Both rooms had balconies and lovely views over the hotel swimming pool, garden, and then out to sea. Lydia's father pointed out the coast of Turkey in the distance, and in the opposite direction they were just able to see the cruise ship which he captained, anchored a little way out from the shore.

'I will try to be here with you as much as possible, but there will be a few times when I have to go to the ship. I wanted you to be somewhere restful and quiet, not on the ship, which is like a large, floating and often very noisy city,' he told them. 'Now I suggest we go to the lounge and have a cup of tea and a cake before you unpack and get settled. Afterwards there will be time for you to explore the hotel grounds and investigate the activities they offer, before dinner.'

Lydia had brought her wheelchair, but as much as possible was using two crutches to help her walk, so tasks like unpacking were not easy, but she was determined that Hannah should not have to take care of her all the time. She did her very best to arrange her belongings, then sat on the bed, exhausted. Her broken ribs were healing well, but they still ached at times. Because both legs were in plaster casts they felt heavy, especially the right leg which had had the metalwork inserted, but thankfully the fractures were healing well and she no longer experienced so much pain.

She took out her smartphone, which told her 'welcome to Greece', then looked on her Instagram and Facebook pages to see if there were any messages, before taking a photo of the room and writing that she was on holiday. The police had warned the girls not to post the actual destination of the holiday or any photos of the beach which might identify where they were, in view of the death threat Lydia had received.

Within a few minutes of posting her news, Lydia had received twenty 'likes' – and she really wished she could tell her digital friends where she actually was staying and how beautiful Samos was.

'Isn't this a fantastic place?' commented Hannah. 'I've never been anywhere like this before. Your mum and dad are so kind to invite me. Do you feel up to walking or being pushed around the garden and swimming pool? I can't wait to explore, and want to enjoy every minute we have.'

'Yes, I can't wait to see it all. It's so exciting to be here and not to have to worry all the time about locking up and things like that. I wish I could go in the pool and have a swim – I'll take my sketchbook and pencils, though, if you want a dip,' she told her friend.

'It's OK – for now let's just explore together,' answered Hannah.

They walked slowly through the terrace at the back of the hotel. The floor was tiled and it was a bit slippery for Lydia on her crutches, but she was determined to walk. A few people were sitting in armchairs, enjoying cool drinks and chatting. A couple looked up and smiled as the girls walked past them and continued down a slope which led into a lovely garden. Even so late in the season, the bougainvillea was still flowering, and there were bushes with red and pink hibiscus flowers as well.

Hannah plucked a blossom and put it behind Lydia's ear. 'You still look beautiful, Lyd,' she commented. 'Your scars are beginning to fade already and your wig is so good that it looks like your real hair.'

'I feel a wreck and I hate to look in a mirror, but then I remind myself that I'm lucky to be alive. I haven't told anyone this, but when I was unconscious, I seemed to be in a very bright place. It was beautiful, so incredibly beautiful that I wanted to stay there forever. Everywhere was bright with gorgeous shimmering colours. I think I must have been dying. Then I remember a voice telling me, very gently, that it wasn't time for me to leave earth yet – people were asking God for me to live – lots of people were praying for me to recover. That's when I woke up and you were by my bed. You won't tell anyone, will you? I don't want people to laugh at me or to think I've got religious, but I now do believe there really is a God, and when I am back to normal I want to start to go to a church. Your mum goes every week, doesn't she? Do you think she would take me with her?' asked Lydia.

'I was one of those who prayed for you – you've always been my best friend and I begged God to let you live. I haven't been to church with my parents for ages. I stopped going when I left junior school, but your accident made me think again. The only thing I could do was to pray, and it was a miracle that you lived and your brain wasn't damaged, as the doctors warned us it could be. When you start to go to church, I'll come with you. I've always believed in God deep down and I promised Him that day you were run over, that if you got better, I would start to go back to church. I promise I won't tell anyone what you have told me – it will be our secret,' answered Hannah.

The swimming pool was gorgeous – so blue and sparkling – but when Hannah put her hand in she was surprised at how cold it was. 'Wow!' she laughed. 'I thought the water would be warm, but it's freezing. I don't think I would want to swim today, anyway.'

At the back of the garden the girls found a play area, meant for smaller children or families. However, there was a huge Connect Four game, and Jenga. There were swings, too, and Lydia managed to sit on one and swing gently.

'I think this will be a fun place – even I will be able to play the games if I sit in my wheelchair,' Lydia said, happily. They stayed on the swings for quite a while, and then were disturbed by a group of young people coming over to them. They looked as if they were in their late teens or early twenties and they were wearing T-shirts bearing the logo of the hotel.

'Hi, there,' said one of the lads. 'I'm Mike, and this is my twin brother, Dave. Are you new guests? We're the sports team here. You can take part in any of the water sports – sailing, surfing, windsurfing, paddle boarding, kayaking – we'll be here to help you. There are also mountain bikes and tennis coaching. It's all free, included in the holiday.'

'I'm Lydia, and this is Hannah,' replied Lydia. 'Sadly, I won't be able to take part in any of those things – but I'm sure Hannah will love to. She's always been a good swimmer, haven't you, Han?'

'I would love to have a go at some of the sports,' answered Hannah. 'I've not tried any of them before, so would be an absolute beginner, but I wouldn't leave Lydia on her own for long. That wouldn't be much fun for her.'

'That's fine – we have our instructor's certificates, so teach people at all levels. If one of the team is free, then they can chill out with Lydia while you are on the water,' suggested Mike, and Hannah smiled in response. He was such a cool-looking guy, maybe late teens, and had a lovely smile. She thought she would like to get to know him better.

The two friends chatted to the girls and guys from the watersports team for quite a long time. Fortunately, most of them were wearing their name badges on their T-shirts, which made it easier for them to remember who they were. The twins seemed to be the leaders, and the girls learned that they were working with the company through a gap year before they went to university.

'When the season here ends,' Dave told them, 'Mike will be taking a bit of time off then he'll go to the French Alps to a ski resort for the winter season until the end of April. He'll get a month off then, and return here for next summer, but I'm leaving at the end of the season to start at uni. When we had our A level results, we both obtained good enough grades for our courses. Mike's decided to start a year later than me,' he added.

'What will you be studying?' asked Hannah, looking at Mike with admiration in her eyes.

'No surprises, really – I'm hoping to study sport science,' Mike told them. 'I have places reserved for next year at both Bath and Loughborough universities. Taking another year out means I can finish some of the training to be a teacher in both winter sports and more of the watersports. It will look good on my CV as well as being fun. I'm a bit of a fun-loving guy,' he told them with a grin. Hannah grinned back – just her kind of guy!

Lydia looked shyly at Dave and asked, 'And you? What do you hope to study?'

'My option is medicine,' he answered. 'Eventually I think I would like to be in General Practice – but that's a long way ahead. It takes seven years of study and training to qualify as a doctor – that's why I wanted to get started this year.'

'Have you always wanted to do medicine?' one of the girls on the sports team asked.

'No,' answered Dave. 'I didn't really know what I wanted to do with my life until I began my A levels. Then I met this amazing older man who is an eye surgeon and works in Uganda. He has saved or restored the sight of so many people there that it made me stop and think. I decided that if I could get the grades needed, then I would apply to a medical school and train as a doctor. I guess I want my life to count for something.'

'How about you girls?' Mike asked, looking at Hannah. Lydia caught his look and thought that he might be attracted to her friend, who blushed slightly and told him about her good GCSE results.

'I've known for a long time that I want to study music,' said Hannah. 'I have played both the flute and the piano since I was seven. The flute is my first love, but you need to have at least grade eight in more than one instrument these days to get a place in a good music school, unless you are a real genius. I'm not, but I would love to be a music teacher in a senior school, eventually. I'm doing grade eight in both instruments and in music theory, as well as my A levels, so I hope I'll do well enough to get a place,' was Hannah's reply.

'How about you, Lydia?' asked Dave. 'What are you hoping to do with your life?'

Lydia paused for a moment, then decided to tell the group about her accident.

'I was really looking forward to going to the sixth form college with Hannah and the rest of our group of friends, but on the last day of term I was run down by a hit-and-run driver and the injuries were pretty severe. Most of the summer holidays I was in hospital and since then I've been struggling to get mobile again. When we go back after the holiday I'm expecting to have the ironwork out of this leg,' she said, patting her right side, 'and hopefully, these casts can come off and I can get around again without the crutches and wheelchair.

'My life has changed totally,' continued Lydia, 'and because of the risk of an epileptic fit at any time, I'm always to be accompanied wherever I go, but we hope that will stabilise eventually,' she added. 'I'm on drugs which still need to be adjusted from time to time as my brain recovers from the trauma. Apparently, it can take up to two years for that to happen, but at least I have hope that in the end, I will be able to do things on my own again. I honestly don't know what I want to do with my life. If I continue to be epileptic then some careers won't be open to me. After being in hospital all that time I think I might like to be a nurse, but that may not be possible. After all that's happened, I just want to get back to college.'

The group of young people made sympathetic noises and several said they would try to help Lydia enjoy her holiday. Lydia looked at her watch – it was almost dinner time. The time had gone by so quickly, chatting to the sports team. However, it took her ages to get changed so she excused herself, and Hannah helped her off the swing and gave her the crutches and the two girls started back to their room. It had been fun meeting the group and the twins seemed especially friendly. As they changed for the evening meal, they talked about the encounter.

'Wow!' said Hannah. 'Isn't Mike gorgeous? He's so cool! I hope he gets to be my teacher when I start trying some sports!'

'Watch out,' said Lydia, teasingly. 'We've always been told that holiday romances don't last.'

Hannah went pink and giggled. 'I wouldn't mind getting to know him a bit more – he's really a cool guy!'

Chapter eight

Lydia and Hannah had fun choosing from the menu at dinner. The meal was laid out as a buffet, with members of the catering staff looking after each dish and serving guests. Some of the food looked very unfamiliar, and so they asked questions and decided to taste a little of each. Apart from moussaka, they didn't know any Greek dishes.

When it came to dessert, the array was mouth-watering.

'Look at those gorgeous little pastries,' Hannah said, when they went to the counter. 'I must try one – it looks like filo pastry and is dripping with honey.'

She helped herself to one while Lydia chose some Greek yoghurt and peaches.

'One thing we're not doing on this holiday is counting calories,' decided Hannah. 'I'll have to make sure I do lots of sports or I will get fat!'

Lydia's parents told them that each evening after dinner there was entertainment of some sort for the guests to enjoy. That first evening it was Greek dancing, and tired though she was, Lydia decided to stay up and watch the display.

She sat with her parents in a shady corner of the terrace, sipping cola and watching a small group of Greek young people dance. The guests were clapping along to the music and enjoying watching them, but then they started to get others to come and join them. The young people of the sports team were soon on their feet and dancing – they had become used to the programme over the summer months.

Once they had danced a routine, they went to bring other guests on to the floor. Mike came over and took Hannah's hand and guided her to the line of dancers. Giggling, she managed, almost on tiptoe, to put her arms over Mike's head and then over Dave's shoulders and copy the steps. The line of dancers made themselves into a circle and one by one they split from the circle and danced on their own in the middle. Hannah, being musical, and light on her feet as well, did her twirls beautifully and was applauded by the audience. Mike gave her a wolf-whistle of appreciation, and she went very pink. Lydia took some photos on her phone and posted them on Instagram – getting several 'likes' from their friends within a few minutes of sending them.

At the end of the evening, while Hannah had a cool drink with her new friends, Lydia's father helped her to her room and then her mum helped her to wash and undress. How she longed to have a cool shower, but that wasn't possible with both legs in plaster. Once she had taken her medication she fell fast asleep, and didn't stir when Hannah crept into the room half an hour later.

'We'll have to be careful that Lydia doesn't overdo things,' Jane commented to her husband as they went to bed. 'She'll hate missing out on any activity, but we were warned that too much excitement could cause another fit. I'm a bit worried.'

'I know, and I agree,' said John, 'but here she should be safe and hopefully begin to put the past few months behind her. I want her to have great memories of Samos which she can treasure all her life. I just hope that the person who tried to kill her will soon be caught and put behind bars for a very long time. Then I'll sleep more soundly, and I guess you will, too. That's why I will be working sometimes while we are here – I want to finish my assignment as soon as I can. I've put you all through too much, and I'm deeply sorry for that.'

'We do understand, John,' answered Jane, 'and neither of us blames you for what happened. We're proud of you and all you do to expose evil practices. I guess I've just felt so fearful for such a long time that all I want now is for us to be a normal, happy family again.'

The only person to wake early next morning was Hannah. She was so excited about being in Samos that she couldn't bear to stay in bed. She tiptoed to the shower and decided to have an early morning swim in the pool, even though the water would be cold. Only once before had she left the shores of Britain, and that was on a school trip to France. Her family were not very well-off and holidays were usually spent with various relatives who lived in the country or by the sea. Not that Hannah ever minded this, for she loved all her aunts and uncles and her grandparents – but she was determined to make the most of this holiday!

As expected, the water in the pool was cool in the early morning, but being a strong swimmer she swam several lengths and quickly became warm.

Hannah felt as if she were glowing all over when she climbed out of the pool and wrapped her towel around her. She was surprised when she heard a voice behind her.

'Hi, Hannah. You're an early bird today, and I can see you are as good a swimmer as you are a dancer.'

Hannah spun around quickly and saw Mike sitting on a stool at the pool-side bar, sipping a cup of coffee. She gave him a wave.

'Fancy a cup?' he asked, and she nodded shyly, then joined him at the bar.

'I'm dripping rather a lot,' she commented, trying to dry her hair with her towel. 'Sorry about being so soggy.'

'That's no problem. Pool-side bars are used to coping with dripping customers. What would you like? This is on me,' he added.

Hannah asked for a latte and was glad of the warm, milky coffee after her swim.

'What's your programme for today?' Mike asked her. 'I'd like to take you out sailing. It looks as if it will be a calm day.'

'I'm not sure – it depends on Lydia, really. I can't leave her alone too much, it wouldn't be fair. Her parents invited me to come so that she would have company of her own age, and it's hard for her to sit and watch everyone do things that before her accident she would have loved to have done. I would love to learn to sail, though. I have an aunt who lives in Portland and the National Sailing Academy is very near to her home. Sometimes when I'm staying with her we watch the students sailing across the bay.'

'Surely Lydia doesn't need you to babysit her all week?' exclaimed Mike. 'I want to make sure you have some fun while you are here. If she's your best friend then she won't want you to sit around all day.'

Hannah looked at Mike, not quite sure that he was being fair, but then in her thoughts a voice told her: 'One day won't hurt – you deserve some fun – Mike's a decent guy, and really cool!'

'OK,' she answered. 'It's a date.' Then she blushed at that; she hadn't thought about it being a real date. 'What time should I be on the beach?'

Mike grinned. He really liked this spunky girl. 'I'll have the dinghy ready for 10am – we should be back about 2pm, so you can still get lunch. See you then.'

Hannah finished her coffee and went slowly back to her room. She just hoped Lydia would understand, and her mother wouldn't mind staying with her. There was something about Mike which she found irresistible – her insides seemed to melt when he looked at her, and parts of her body began to tingle. She had never felt like this about anyone before – not even when she had been dancing with Joe at the school prom. The couple of dates they had been on since then had been fun, but he felt more like a brother than a boyfriend.

Chapter nine

Lydia was a little disappointed when she heard Hannah's plans, but she tried not to show it. She had hoped that they might have explored the coastline together. She knew her parents would be glad to push her in her wheelchair, but she wanted them to have some time together. They rarely got time just to be a normal couple.

'I'll sit by the pool and read, or maybe sketch a little,' she told her friend. 'And if Dad helps me to the beach, I can watch you sail. You have a good time.'

After breakfast Hannah went to the beach, wearing her new bikini under her shorts and favourite strappy top. Her hair was pulled back into a ponytail and she wore her sunglasses to shield her eyes from the Mediterranean sun. She was glad she was no longer chubby and had a good figure – and she secretly hoped Mike would notice that.

Lydia's parents sat with her by the pool, lazing and sunbathing. They phoned her grandparents and they chatted together. In fact, although she tried to read, Lydia found it gave her a headache and so she put her book down.

Concentration wasn't easy since the accident. She hobbled on her crutches over to the bar and bought an iced tea. It was lovely to sip it slowly. She tried not to feel angry about Hannah, or jealous that she was out sailing and having fun. She knew she should be grateful that she was alive and her brain was not damaged, but it wasn't always easy to feel that way. After a while she asked her father to push her to the beach, which he did gladly. They talked together and he told her again about Valetta harbour and the hours he used to spend just looking out to sea. So many sailing boats were out in the bay, Lydia didn't know which one Hannah was in.

'Would you mind if Mum and I went for a little walk?' asked her dad after a while. 'I promise we won't leave you for long, or be out of your sight or shouting distance if you need us – but we need to stretch our legs.'

'That's fine,' answered Lydia, once again struggling not to show them that it wasn't fine and she didn't want to be alone. She was sitting on a lounger, under an umbrella, with a table by her side. She had her sketching things and started to draw the scene in front of her. To the right, there was the coastline of Samos, and the sea was the most amazing shades of turquoise and blue, misty on the horizon, and there were hills rising from the shore. When she looked to the left she could see the coastline of Turkey, and noticed that the straits between Turkey and Samos were very narrow. There was a patrol boat sailing around the area and a military installation on the Samos side, guarding the coastline. Several sailing boats were in the bay, their sails blowing in the off-shore breeze. Some people were paddle boarding and others windsurfing, so there were loads of things to watch and draw. Soon Lydia became absorbed and forgot her sadness and anger at not being with Hannah.

It seemed that in no time at all her parents had returned and suggested they go to the beach bar and choose a snack for lunch.

The beach bar was full of many of the young watersports instructors who had finished their morning shifts. Glancing around, Lydia looked for Mike – but he wasn't there. She had a momentary worry about Hannah, but quickly dismissed it because she was sure she would be safe with a trained instructor. However, Dave was there, and when he saw Lydia, he came over.

'Hey, there!' he greeted Lydia and her parents. 'What have you been doing this morning?'

'Not a great deal,' Lydia answered honestly. 'I was a bit tired after last night, so we stayed by the pool and on the beach. I did a little sketching.'

'Can I see?' asked Dave, and he bent to her level to admire her drawing.

'That's great,' he said, encouragingly. 'You're an artist – you really have talent.'

'Not much,' she laughed. 'But I do have fun sketching. I've scribbled and painted a bit most of my life. I can't concentrate very well on reading since the accident – it gives me headaches.'

'Tell me more about the accident. What exactly happened?' Dave asked.

Before Lydia could begin to explain, her dad spoke. 'It's still very upsetting for us to talk much about it – Lydia was run over on a pedestrian crossing by a hit-and-run driver at the end of the school term. I was away at sea. Can you see that cruise ship anchored off the bay? That's the ship I captain. I can never forgive myself that I wasn't around when the accident happened. We almost lost our precious daughter and this holiday is to help us forget it for a few days.'

'I'm so sorry, sir,' said Dave. 'I asked without thinking. Please forgive me. I am going back to London soon to study medicine and I had wondered what had happened. I've been amazed to see Lydia's courage and cheerfulness. Would you let me push her along the beach sometime? I promise I won't ask any more questions and I'll take good care of her.'

'If Lydia wants to go, then of course you may. This evening I need to return to my ship and I was thinking of taking the family and Hannah for dinner on board. If you are free, you are welcome to join us. The car will come to collect us at 7pm and will bring the ladies back around 10pm.'

'Hey, that sounds great,' answered Dave. 'It's my evening off and tomorrow is my day off. I'd love to see round the ship – and of course, be with you all and have dinner. Thank you so much. Thanks for inviting me. That's really cool!'

'Dave,' said Lydia, 'I would really love you to take me to explore the beach, but could we do that tomorrow? I'm a bit tired now and ought to get some rest this afternoon if we're going out this evening. We'll see you at reception at 7pm. It's a bit formal at the captain's table for dinner – I need time to get ready slowly. Is that OK with you?'

'Sure – that's great,' he answered, thankful that in her own sweet way Lydia had warned him that he needed to dress up for dinner. He had heard about people having dinner at the captain's table on board ship. He would need to hunt around and find a tie; he hadn't worn one since he came to Samos.

Lydia was lying on her bed dozing when Hannah came in. She had been gone for hours. She looked excited and flushed and was obviously longing to talk and tell her all about her day.

'You look like you had a great time. Ready for a girlie heart-to-heart?' she asked Hannah.

Hannah giggled and blushed. 'It was wicked! The sailing was such fun, and Mike said I'm a natural at it. He wants to take me out every day, but I told him I wouldn't do that – I couldn't leave you alone all the time. He's really fun and I think he likes me. I mean, really likes me. He's hot!'

'Oh, Hannah, I'm glad you got to sail and it was such fun, but be careful – he's a bit older than us, and you don't really know him very well yet. We're only here for a little while and you don't want to go home with a broken heart! I can see you've already got the hots for him!'

'I admit I have. I feel so different when he's around – I feel really alive and excited. Honest, Lyd, my body tingles in places I didn't know existed. When he put his arm around me to help me learn the ropes, his touch was like electricity shooting through my body… I think he felt it too! Do you think this is what love feels like?'

'I'm not sure. After the prom when Sam kissed me, I felt like that. I felt the kiss right through my body, not just on my lips. I thought perhaps he cared about me. I didn't dare to think it could be love. I thought I had the hots for him, too – but when he looked at me after the accident I knew it was just the physical "me" which had attracted him; he loathed what he saw that day. Be careful, Hannah, don't get in so deep that you get hurt like I did. You're my best friend and I don't want you to get hurt.

'By the way, we're going for dinner on Dad's ship this evening,' Lydia informed her. 'We need to dress up for the captain's table. I should have brought my ball dress, but I'll have to make do with a pretty cotton one. What will you wear? Dad's invited Mike's brother, Dave, to join us. A car is coming at 7pm to collect us all.'

'That's exciting. I must text the family about that. I wish Mike was coming with us, too!' added Hannah, with a sigh. 'Can you help me choose something suitable to wear?'

Chapter ten

The young people were excited to visit the cruise ship and, as far as they were concerned, it was a huge success, at least to start with. Since they were the family and friends of the captain, they were treated like royalty. Lydia and her mother had been entertained there several times in the past, but this time was extra special since many of the staff knew about Lydia's terrible accident and wanted the visit to be a special time for her.

They were met at the harbour and taken to the main ship in a dinghy which was normally used to take the passengers to the shore on excursions. As the boat approached the cruise ship, they noticed a long line of sailors standing to attention, and they were piped aboard. Then Jane, Lydia and Hannah were presented with lovely orchid corsages, and John and Dave with buttonholes for their jackets, before being led to John's suite of rooms, where drinks and snacks were served. Lydia asked for her new, favourite drink of iced peach tea, which she had been having since she arrived on Samos. Dave seemed quite at home with everyone and asked John lots of questions about the running of a cruise ship. Lydia's father promised that he would take him to meet the ship's medical staff and see the well-equipped 'hospital' they had on board, should any of the guests or staff need treatment.

'Have you always wanted to be a doctor?' Jane asked Dave.

'I guess I didn't really think about a career much while I was at school,' he told them all. 'Mike and I and our younger brother, Morgan, like most boys, wanted to be footballers, or firemen. Mike is the most athletic of the three of us, so none of us were surprised when he decided to study sports. I've always loved sport but once I got past the stage of wanting to be a footballer, I knew sport would only ever be a hobby for me.

'I was about seventeen when we had a visitor come to stay. He was quite old, about seventy, and had never married. He had lived in East Africa most of his working life and was a specialist eye surgeon. I remember sitting and chatting to him one evening and just being so amazed that he had helped so many blind people to see. Also, he'd trained teams of health assistants and nurses, who then were able to go back to their own towns and villages and perform simple operations like removal of cataracts, giving people back their sight.

'I think that was the turning point for me. I knew I wanted to help people and make a difference in the world. That sounds a bit dramatic, doesn't it? I don't mean it in that way, but I do want my life to count for something. It spurred me on to really study hard for my A levels – and I was so thrilled when I had good results and was granted a place at University College London. It will be years of hard work before I qualify, but I don't mind that. My parents have been supportive and encouraging, too.'

Lydia's parents were so impressed by Dave's story, just as she and Hannah had been, and felt sure he would succeed and one day become a great doctor.

'What about Morgan?' asked Hannah. 'You haven't mentioned him before. How old is he and what does he want to do?'

'Morgan is the same age as you girls. He took his GCSEs this year and did quite well. It's harder for him because he's dyslexic – but he wants to do A levels in Maths, Art and Photography. He takes amazing photos and Dad has built him a studio at the very top of our house. We actually don't live in a regular house – it's a converted windmill near Ely, so Morgan's room and studio are right at the top where the sails were. It's a great place for him to work. Well, we all love the old windmill – it's not a huge house for a family of five, but we are so proud of it because our dad did the conversion and renovation himself. At the back, there's a small extension with a modern kitchen for Mum. While it was being built, we somehow all managed to squeeze into a mobile home, and we lived on site for two years. That was a challenge for us all. We were smaller, of course, but we had quite a menagerie of pets living in hutches, and a kennel for our dog, as well. I think it must have been quite hard for Mum, but I don't remember her complaining. Dad is an architect and he kept up with work in his office in Ely while he built our house.'

'That sounds amazing,' commented Lydia. 'Fancy living in a windmill – I only ever remember seeing one, not far from us in Shirley, but I haven't heard of anyone living in one. It makes our suburban semi sound very ordinary.'

Soon they were called to the dining room and were treated to a wonderful meal. Hannah, Lydia and Dave took quite a while choosing from the menu because there were so many mouth-watering dishes listed.

After dinner, there was entertainment – in fact, there were several different shows, films, dances and bands for them to choose from. Captain Rocco suggested they went to a light classical concert which Hannah would especially enjoy, as she hoped to have a career in music. While they were in the concert hall enjoying the music, the weather began to change, and by the time the concert had ended they were in the middle of a thunderstorm. The cruise ship was large, but it was moving up and down with the increased swell of the sea.

'I think you had all better stay on board until the storm passes,' Lydia's father told them. 'Although we're not far off shore, the seas around here can be treacherous.'

Dave looked concerned. 'I would like to get back as soon as possible, Captain Rocco,' he said. 'Almost every night there are migrants trying to get across from Turkey, and even in fairly good weather some of the boats have capsized. Mike and I and some of the other experienced watersports team go out in the dinghies to see if we can help, in case they are in trouble. Now that winter is approaching there have been even more migrants trying to cross before the bad weather comes.'

'I was already thinking of ordering some of my lifeboats and crew out – would you like to join them? Afterwards I'll make sure you get back to the hotel safely. Jane and the girls can go back as soon as the storm subsides a little,' John suggested.

'I'll try to contact my brother and tell him what's happening. The storm is so bad that the team would be better not going out in our small sailing boats – your lifeboats would be a much safer option. I'm very grateful for your offer,' Dave replied. 'Hey, girls, I'm sorry to leave you, but I've seen some of the migrants in trouble when the sea hasn't been half as rough as it is now. Take care, and we'll meet up tomorrow. It's been a great evening, thanks so much.'

Lydia's father soon had his crew organised and three lifeboats were lowered, with Dave in the first of them. It was a night that would continue to live within the memories of them all, although for many of the passengers on the ship it was just a normal night of enjoyment, and they were hardly aware of the noise of the thunder and the power of the lightning outside. Up on the deck it was a different story. The wind was blowing and the waves were huge as the sailors lowered the lifeboats. The flashes of lightning lit up the sky and the cracks of thunder were loud, almost instantaneous with the lightning. Only three lifeboats could be spared. Captain Rocco knew he must keep enough in reserve should his passengers need them, even though the ship should weather the storm without any problem.

Dave sped over the bay in the lifeboat, which was steered by the chief mate. He was glad of the experience of the sailors, and that he had been allowed to help in the rescue. The lifeboat was well equipped with foil blankets to keep any survivors warm, as well as water, food and flasks of hot drinks and medical supplies. The ship's doctor was with them, plus one nurse – medical staff had also been distributed in the other two boats. The sky was pitch black apart from the bursts of lightning every few minutes. The cracks of thunder were unnerving, too – and the lifeboat was pitching and tossing. Dave was normally a good sailor, but even he began to feel sick and felt a fear that seemed to make his throat constrict with terror. He had a good life jacket around him and a powerful waterproof torch in his pocket. He wondered how the migrants must feel in overcrowded, unseaworthy dinghies and with no proper equipment. They were never provided with enough life jackets for the number of passengers. They must be utterly terrified! It made his blood boil to think about the exploitation of the people traffickers and their complete disregard of human life.

Soon they were over the bay and close to the Turkish coast. They sighted a dinghy and, even above the noise of the wind, waves and thunder, they could hear people screaming. Suddenly, they were aware of people around the lifeboat, floating in the sea. Work began in earnest as they tried to rescue as many as possible. Sadly, as well as distressed people, there were bodies of some migrants who had perished. Because of lack of space in the boat, the living had to have priority.

Just as they were about to turn around and take their full boat back to the cruise ship, Dave spotted another person struggling in the sea. His torch showed him that the person was holding a small child and flailing around in desperation. He had no option – he could not reach her from within the safety of the lifeboat, so with a quick word to the chief mate to wait for him, he dived into the pitch-black sea and swam to the person.

It was a girl, holding a dead child. Using all the strength he could muster and with a silent prayer for help, he began to hold her and swim backstroke to the boat. Strong arms pulled them both to safety and wrapped them in foil. He put his arm around the girl and tried to gently pull away the dead child, but she was sobbing and would not let go. Tears were rolling down his own face at the sadness and horror of the situation.

Altogether that night, fifty-three migrants were saved by the crew of the cruise ship. Many more were lost. A patrol boat had rescued a few more people – and a very small number had, by some miracle, managed to swim to the shore where they were found by local people, who helped them. All the migrants who were well enough were looked after in one of the ship's lounges for the night, and the next day would be taken to Samos town, the capital of the island, to be interviewed and admitted to the refugee camp, until their futures could be sorted out.

Those who were very sick were taken at once to the shore and ambulances were waiting to take them to the main hospital, which was in the town of Samos. Dave had been so upset by the young girl he had rescued, who for a long time would not let go of the dead baby, that he asked if he could accompany her to the hospital. He explained that on his free days at the hotel he had been visiting the refugee camp and trying to help the migrants – he felt so sorry about their plight and so angry about the issue of people smuggling. He knew that she would need to know about the baby, who had been given a swift, but reverent, burial at sea.

Chapter eleven

Captain Rocco planned to briefly return to shore. His intention had been, as soon as the storm abated a little, to see his family and Hannah safely into the car which would take them back to the hotel, and then to return to his ship. He wanted to talk with the survivors. If any were able to speak English, then they might be able to help him with his investigative journalistic work, which was to expose and catch people smugglers.

However, his plans quickly changed. They had all transferred safely down the rope ladder, which was a real challenge in the wind, into the tug boat, and set off for the shore, when there was a terrific display of sheet lightning, almost blinding them. This lightning was so bright that it triggered an epileptic fit in Lydia's brain. Once again, she felt terrified as her body began to writhe and shake, and she couldn't think clearly or control anything. Her dad and mum managed to lie her down and put her into the recovery position on her side, after which she became unconscious and deathly pale. Hannah was terrified and began to pray for God to help them. She feared once again for her friend's life.

As soon as they reached the shore, her father carried her to one of the waiting ambulances and they were driven to the hospital in Samos town. Even with the help of the ambulance crew, Lydia was still unconscious and her pulse was weak. She was rushed to the Intensive Care Unit and wired up to a life-support machine.

Once again, her mum, dad and Hannah were sitting around her bed and silently praying that she would recover. How could it have happened again? It was true that the medical staff at the Atkinson Morley Hospital had warned them of long-lasting complications from her brain injuries – that was the reason why Lydia needed someone near her all the time, in case she had a fit – but she had been so well since her discharge, they had all become a bit complacent.

It was a long, long night. Hannah remembered her promise to God last time when Lydia was so ill – she had promised to let God into her life and go to church again with her parents – but she hadn't yet done so. Hannah cried, and whispered a prayer once again to God, begging Him to forgive her and to heal Lydia. Then she wrote a text message to her mum, asking her to pray.

It was difficult being in a hospital where everyone spoke Greek and not many people could speak more than a few words in English. All the staff were very busy, as several migrants who had been rescued from the sea were very sick indeed and required intensive care. Sheer weariness took over, and Hannah and Lydia's parents eventually dozed off as they sat around the bed, in spite of all the noise going on in the unit. They were woken up stiff, cold and thirsty, by the noise of voices near them. Three doctors were discussing Lydia's condition. When they saw that her parents were waking, one of them was able to explain in English that all Lydia's vital signs were now stable, but they were not sure why she had not yet regained consciousness, but as soon as she did, she would be taken to a female ward for observation. They suggested that the family go back to the hotel and recover and promised to phone as soon as there was any change in Lydia's condition. Jane wasn't sure about leaving Lydia, but since she couldn't speak Greek, John persuaded her that they would all be better able to help Lydia if they went back to the hotel and got some sleep.

A taxi took them back and they were met by the hotel staff, who were so kind. Soon they were fed, showered and able to sleep. One of the staff members was an Englishwoman who was married to a Greek, and she was fluent in the Greek language. She promised Lydia's parents that she would go with them to the hospital and translate for them later in the day. That was a great relief.

'Hannah,' Lydia's mum said, 'take today off and try to relax and have some fun. We'll go back to the hospital. Lydia will need your company when she's recovered a bit. We'll text you all the news.'

After a good sleep, even though she didn't really feel like it, Hannah took the advice, changed into her bikini and went down to the pool. A swim made her feel a bit better, so she ventured to the beach and watched the sailing and paddle boarding. The sports team were all busy instructing, but after they had finished they went for lunch at the poolside bar, and Mike spotted Hannah on his way up.

'Hi, Hannah,' he called. 'How are things this morning? Dave told me about the rough night you've had. He's down at the hospital now, visiting a young girl he rescued last night. It's his day off today. I'm so sorry to hear about Lydia. Are you free to come and have some lunch with me?'

Hannah looked up and saw the kindness in Mike's face. She was feeling lonely and thoughts of last night kept circling through her mind, so she agreed. She was quiet most of the time, but Mike didn't seem to mind – he seemed to understand how traumatised she felt. He told her how Dave had helped with the rescue and come back very late, totally exhausted.

When they had finished eating, Mike asked Hannah if she felt OK – and she nodded. 'Then why don't we take a walk along the beach?' he suggested. 'I have a whole hour before I have a windsurfing lesson to supervise.'

'Thanks, I'd like that,' agreed Hannah. 'It might stop my mind from going round and round in circles, thinking about Lydia. I wanted to go back to the hospital with her parents, but they told me to wait until she's feeling better, then I can keep her company.'

Mike reached out and took her hand, and it made her feel warm and tingly. She looked up at him and smiled. Suddenly she found her tongue and began to talk about the evening before – all the fun they had before the storm broke.

Mike didn't interrupt – he let Hannah talk, knowing instinctively that it would help her. A mile or so from the hotel they were both shocked as they saw several life jackets which had been washed up on the beach, or maybe abandoned by migrants once they reached land. It brought home to them, once again, the reality of the plight which the migrants faced – boat-loads of them every day, trying to escape from war-torn Syria or other countries where they faced persecution or disaster.

Hannah and Mike stopped at a small beachside café and had a cold drink – looking at a now calm and beautiful bay, and watching a Turkish military boat patrolling the area.

'Dave has been visiting the migrants in the refugee camp,' explained Mike. 'He's a much more serious guy than me. I've been the one wanting a good time – not really focusing on my studies as much as I should. We're only young once and my philosophy has been to have fun and get away with as little work as possible, but it isn't that I don't care. Underneath I get really upset when I see things like those life jackets. I try to help with the rescues, but feel pretty helpless most of the time.'

'I understand that,' replied Hannah. 'I sit with Lydia, talking to her, not knowing if she hears me, feeling utterly helpless. I cry out to God to help – I hope *He* hears me.'

'Tell me about Lydia's accident,' Mike said.

Hannah took a deep breath and launched into the whole story – from the end of the exams, the prom, and then the hit-and-run accident. She told him of the weeks of waiting for the medical staff to bring Lydia out of the induced coma, and then their joy that her main brain functions seemed to be intact. 'Her broken ribs now seem to be all healed and her legs are soon to come out of plaster and should be alright. She will have scars on them because she had what are called compound fractures, where the broken bones have pushed through the skin. The face wounds will fade a bit, but everyone worries about the brain healing completely, and hopes she won't suffer from epilepsy for the rest of her life. She's been so brave and most of the time, very cheerful, but I think this episode will upset her a lot. She is so hoping to go to college after Christmas. Missing one whole term will be bad enough, she'll have so many lessons to catch up with.'

Lydia woke up and had no idea where she was or what had happened. All she could hear was the ticking and buzzing of monitors and people speaking in a language she didn't understand. She tried to focus her eyes – then as she looked, she realised she was in a hospital ward, but it wasn't the one she had been in before. Her head ached, so she closed her eyes again and tried to lie still. After a little while she heard footsteps near her bed so she opened her eyes again. This time she could see a little more – there was a nurse looking at her monitors and then she looked at Lydia and smiled. Lydia smiled back. The nurse spoke to her, but Lydia didn't understand.

'I'm English,' she said. Her throat was dry and sore from the tube which had been put into it.

The nurse nodded and said, 'Good,' before walking away to fetch someone who could help. She came back with a doctor, who spoke to Lydia.

'Good girl. Now you wake up! Does your head hurt?' he asked, pointing to her head.

Lydia touched her head and was aware that her wig had gone. Her hair was short and didn't feel right. She tried to nod to the doctor as she answered, 'Yes.'

'I phone your father and mother to come – soon you will be well,' he told her.

'Thank you,' she answered. 'Where am I?'

The doctor smiled and reminded her that she was in Samos. It took a minute or two to register, then she remembered she was on holiday, but even thinking about that made her head ache again, so she closed her eyes.

'Good girl,' said the doctor once more. 'Now sleep a little – soon we take the machines away.'

Lydia's parents were thrilled to hear the good news when the doctor phoned them to say that Lydia had woken up and was talking.

'You may come and visit. Tomorrow we will take her to a ward. She will soon be well again.'

Hannah was still on the walk with Mike when the good news was phoned through to Lydia's parents, so Jane sent her a text message to say that Lydia had woken up and she and John were going to sit with her, but she had to be kept very quiet until her head stopped hurting. She promised Hannah that she could visit the following day, when Lydia should be back in a normal ward.

The message cheered Hannah and Mike, and they walked back, hand in hand, to the hotel. Mike went to do his shift teaching windsurfing.

'Do you fancy having ago at it?' he asked her. 'The other two people who signed up are beginners, so you wouldn't feel out of your depth.'

The exercise was great and made her feel better – it was amazing to feel the wind blowing through her hair and in her face, and with Mike's strong arms around her she felt safe and exhilarated all at the same time. There was no doubt about it, she had feelings for Mike – but he had told her he was a fun-loving boy. Something in Hannah's mind told her Lydia had been right to warn her to be careful. Maybe he was just amusing himself with her. What would her mum and dad think? They had also warned her about boys who just wanted to use girls for their own fun, and then dumped them. Was Mike just being nice to her because she was a pretty girl, or did he really like her for herself? The question kept popping into her mind.

Chapter twelve

Lydia was immensely relieved when all the wires and tubes were removed from her body and she was taken to a women's ward. Her head was still feeling a bit fuzzy, making thinking difficult, but she knew she was on the mend and hopefully she would soon be back at the hotel. Most of the people in the ward were older women, chatting away to each other in Greek. Next to her was a dark-skinned girl with Afro hair, who looked very sad and wasn't communicating with anyone. Lydia tried to speak to her – she knew almost no Greek, but did know that '*kalimera*' meant 'good morning', so she tried that. There was no response. Then she tried again, in English.

'Hello, I'm Lydia,' she said.

A faint smile came over the girl's face, showing that she understood. 'Hello,' she replied. 'I'm Nakato. You speak English? I learned English at school.' Nakato gave a big sigh and tears began to roll down her face.

'What is the matter?' asked Lydia, upset to see the girl's distress. 'If you tell me, then maybe my parents would be able to help. They will come later and see me.'

Nakato looked thoughtfully at Lydia, wondering if she could trust this stranger. There were so few people she had found trustworthy, and now she was in yet another strange country and didn't know what would happen to her. For a few moments she was silent, then she decided to take the risk.

'Lydia, if I tell you my story, it will take a long time, but I do need help and advice. I just don't know what I am to do. Are you willing to listen?'

'I'll try,' answered Lydia. 'If my head starts to ache again, then I'll ask you to stop for a while – but it won't be because I don't want to know your story. It will just mean I need a rest.'

'OK,' said Nakato. 'Then I'll begin. I'm almost seventeen years old and was born in a village called Amudat in north-west Uganda. My parents were from the Pokot tribe. I was born a twin – my twin sister, Babirye, died as a small baby. All twins in Uganda were called Nakato and Babirye, it's a – what do you call it? – tradition. My parents had a small *shamba* – a garden – where we grew food to eat, and some very much-loved cattle. Cattle are the wealth of the Pokot people. Father had several wives, so I had many older brothers and sisters.

'I was six years old when two bad things happened. First, my mother died giving birth to another baby, who also died. I was then given to one of my father's other wives – she was to bring me up, but she hated me and didn't treat me like her own children, but as a servant. The other bad thing was that cattle raiders came one night and stole our precious cows. Such things happen among the Pokot and Karamojong tribes.

'After these bad things, Father decided to go to the town and try to find work. We all moved a little way to the south, near to the mountain of Elgon, in the Kapchorwa district. He had relatives there. Some of his wives and children stayed to work on the *shamba*, but my stepmother was his favourite wife, so I was taken along with her children to live in a town called Sironko. That was very good for me because my father was a forward-looking man and wanted his children to be educated, so I was sent to school along with the children of my stepmother. Yes, I still had to work hard for her and got beaten many times, but I loved school. I was soon top of the class, and it was at that school I learned to speak English. My stepmother was angry because I learned faster than her children, but Father praised me. She couldn't stop me from attending the school, because she might lose favour with my father.

'Life continued in this way until I was eleven years old. I had reached primary five and hoped that I would be able to go to senior school one day, but it was not to be. Although my father believed in education, even for girls, he still believed strongly in the tribal traditions. He sent me away to Grandmother for a time, to have the things done to me that a girl needed before she could be married.' Nakato paused and gave another long sigh. 'That was when the real trouble began.'

'What do you mean?' Lydia asked. 'What had to be done when you were eleven years old?'

'In our tradition, girls have to be cut down below, where babies come out. I understand now, but then nobody told me what was happening. Grandmother held me down and a woman in her village, whose job it is to cut girls, used a razor and cut away a big piece of flesh. I screamed – the pain was terrible – and I bled a lot. I was taken to Grandmother's hut and rags with some herbs were put on me like a bandage. It took some weeks to heal. I was so angry. I wished my own mother had been alive – I felt sure she would not have let anyone hurt me so much. That was just in my mind, because all of Father's daughters had been cut when they were around eleven years old. It was our tradition. I will never forget the pain and horror of that time in the bush with Grandmother.'

Lydia was shocked. She vaguely remembered hearing something on TV about female circumcision but hadn't really thought about it – it was just something which happened in other cultures. She found tears on her cheeks as she listened to Nakato relating her pain and how horrible it was.

Just then a nurse came around to check the temperatures and pulses of her patients, so the girls stopped talking. After this, the doctors' rounds began. The doctor who spoke a little English seemed pleased with Lydia's progress. He patted her head and said, 'Good girl – you get home soon,' and passed on to the next patient.

The staff seemed pleased that Nakato was at last talking to someone and taking an interest in her surroundings. The nurses helped both girls to get washed and to sit together in chairs near the window. Lydia was pleased; it made it easier to talk to Nakato.

'Please tell me more,' she said. 'Did you go back to school after you were cut?'

'No,' answered Nakato. 'I was very upset. Father said I had learned enough and he would now find me a husband. He had saved enough to buy some cows for my dowry – not many, so I would not be a "first" wife. I cried and cried. The only person who seemed to care about me was the eldest son of my stepmother. He helped me with the chores I had to do, like collecting water from the river, getting firewood and doing the washing. It is shameful for a boy, especially a big boy, to do such things, but he always helped and managed to keep out of sight of his mother, for she would have killed me had she known. His name is Musome. I owe my life to him. He also used to ask me to help him with his homework and so I was still learning. He worked very hard at school and went through to senior school and then had a scholarship to Makerere University in our capital city, Kampala. He is still there and will be a great and good man.

'One day my father and stepmother told me to dress in my best dress, and gave me money to go to the hairdresser and have my hair plaited and beaded. I had the Pokot necklaces around my neck and bangles on my arms. When I was ready I was taken to meet the man who was to be my husband. When I saw him, I was so shocked – he was an old man! I was still eleven and only just developing into a woman – my monthly bleeds had started – so I guess I was old enough to be married. I knew how to keep a hut clean, cook meals and do the chores, but inside I was just a girl and longed to play with my friends.

'The day of the wedding came very soon – far too soon. I was so scared. After the tribal ceremony, I was taken to the bridal hut and hated the time my husband, Abdul, came to me. He was a horrible old man and smelt. He used me when he felt like it, and the rest of the time I served his other wives and was just like a slave. From time to time Musome would come to visit me, bringing little gifts. Without him, my life would have been unbearable. He was the only one who cared enough to visit me or ask how I was.

'"Don't worry, little sister," he would say each time he went away. "I will always look after you." That gave me hope. He told me one day that he didn't believe in the Moslem god, Allah, anymore – he was learning about the Christian faith from some of his friends. He told me about love – something I didn't really know about, except through his caring attitude. We could talk together in English, because no one else could understand that language. If the family knew what he was thinking and saying, they would kill him. It would bring such shame on our family. It was easy to go to the witchdoctor and get poison if you hated somebody!

'When I was thirteen I became pregnant. I was so scared! My husband had moved us all to a town in Kenya called Kapenguria – still within the Pokot tribal area. It felt strange to be living in another country, even though the tribal language and culture was the same. Musome still came to visit, as people could have a white paper which allowed them to cross the border easily. When I grew big with the baby, he brought me gifts of food and even some clothes to wrap the baby in when it was born. When my time drew near, I was taken to the hut of my mother-in-law – that was where I was to deliver, and she would act as midwife. She had delivered all her grandchildren, and although she was an old, old woman, she had a kindness about her.

'She gave me rags to bite on when the pains came. It took many hours before the baby was ready to be born. The pain of the delivery was terrible – I was still young and small and the baby tore me badly as he came out. I called him Musome to honour my stepbrother, but his official name was Mohammed, named by my husband. I thought my husband would be pleased with me as I had given him a son, but I never healed from the birth and began to leak urine all the time. I became an outcast in my husband's family. Nobody wanted to come near me.

'I loved my baby and tried to feed him and take care of him. The only person who gave me advice was my mother-in-law, but even she hated the urine smell.

'"Don't blame me," she said one day, in anger. "All my grandchildren were born without problems. You must be a cursed girl." One day my baby became sick and my husband took him to the traditional doctor. He killed a chicken and put the blood on him and said Musome was cursed because I leaked urine. I cried and begged Abdul to take him to a proper hospital, but he got angry, beat me and refused. My precious baby died when he was just three months old. I wished I had died with him. I felt miserable – an outcast with no future. No one wanted me near them, my husband now despised me because I could not give him another baby. Most days I was sent to the fields to work, given little food and had to stay alone in an old hut at night.

'Musome, my stepbrother, was very angry. He kept his promise and continued to visit me when he could, but it was a long way because he was now studying engineering in Kampala, and so that he could get money, he worked when he wasn't at school. He told his new Christian friends about me and they asked their God, Jesus, to help me.

'One day he came and he had a plan. "Nakato," he said, "the university vacation is coming and my friends have helped me make a plan for you to escape and get treatment. We have all saved up money to help you. My friends have asked people in their churches to give money, too."

'Can you believe that? People who I had never met, and who were not even from our tribe or family, gave money to help me escape to a new life – such a thing I had never heard of in all my life!'

A nurse came towards the two girls. She smiled at them and indicated that it was time to eat. She helped Lydia with her crutches and then took her to the loo. Lydia was grateful – she hated using the bedpans, which the nurses had brought when she was in the Intensive Care Unit. Next, it was Nakato's turn and the nurse helped her, giving her clean pads to wear. Lydia was sad to see that her problem was still there. At least in hospital she could be helped to keep clean and dry and not be smelly all the time. Lydia thought about how she had wrinkled up her nose if some old person had got on a bus and they smelt a bit unsavoury. How unkind she had been – maybe they had no one to help them with their problem, either.

94

Chapter thirteen

After lunch, the girls were put back on their beds to rest. It was the rule for everyone. This Greek hospital seemed very strict about rules. The ward had to be quiet for an hour. In a way, Lydia was glad. She needed to absorb the sad story she was hearing, even though she was curious to know what happened next.

Hannah had wanted to go and visit Lydia that morning, but Jane told her that the hospital had rules and the visiting time was restricted now that Lydia was out of danger. So she decided to go to the beach. Mike and the team were in action, giving lessons.

'Hi, Hannah, would you like to try sailing again today?' Mike asked her.

'I'd love to,' she replied, 'but I need to have lunch in good time so that I can visit Lydia this afternoon.'

It was huge fun, and she learned that there would be a regatta soon and she would be able to take part in that. Even though Mike had other clients to take sailing and windsurfing, he always seemed to give her a special smile and encouragement – almost as if she were his girlfriend. She wished she was, but tried to keep reminding herself that in a few days she would be going home and back to college, and Mike would most likely forget all about her. She thought of Joe, who had been her beau at the school prom and wanted to be her boyfriend – indeed, she had thought of him in that way until she met Mike. Joe had never made her tingle all over when he held her hand. He was a nice boy, but nothing compared to the gorgeous hunk of a man that Mike was! Mike had taken off his T-shirt and she couldn't help but admire his rippling muscles and tanned skin. She would really like to know him better!

'Penny for your thoughts,' said Mike, startling her from her reverie.

Hannah blushed. 'Nothing, really,' she said. 'Just thinking that I have to go home in a few days.'

'Forget it!' said Mike, brightly. 'Enjoy the time you have here. I've got an evening off, why don't I take you to the harbour at Pythagoreio? It's such a great place to hang out for an evening, and not far from here. You've not seen anything much except this beach.'

Hannah felt excited, but wasn't sure. 'I need to see what time we get back from the hospital, and should ask if Lydia's parents are OK with the idea. They are responsible for me while I'm here – in fact, they paid for me to come along and keep Lydia company,' she answered. Mike pulled a face, making her laugh, and she promised to give him an answer at dinner.

Hannah showered and changed into her shorts and T-shirt and went to the pool café to meet John and Jane for lunch. Then they hired a taxi to take them to the hospital.

When Hannah entered the ward, it was such a relief to see Lydia sitting up in a chair and looking heaps better – although she was still missing her wig. However, her own hair was growing back, so she didn't look too bald.

'Tomorrow I am to have a brainwave test – an EEG, the doctor called it – and if that is normal then I can be discharged,' she told them, excitedly.

'That's wonderful, darling,' exclaimed her father. 'I have to go back to the ship tomorrow and she needs to sail on to the next port of call – I'll be much happier if I know you're back at the hotel. When she's settled at her next mooring, I'll try to come back here and have another day or so together with you all, before you leave to go home. I've got some rather pressing business which I have to attend to, otherwise I would just stay with you all the time.'

'What have you been doing, Hannah?' Lydia asked her friend. Hannah told her about her sailing and windsurfing lessons and her walk along the beach with Mike. She told her how upset she had been to see the life jackets on the shore.

'It was horrible to see those life jackets,' she told them all. 'I only hope that the people who wore them managed to get safely to shore. Mike told me about Dave helping on the lifeboat.'

Then it seemed a good time to ask Lydia's parents if she could go to Pythagoreio with Mike after dinner.

'He will take good care of you, Hannah, won't he?' asked Lydia's mum. 'I hate to put a curfew on you, but I would be happy to know that you are back at the hotel by midnight. It may seem a bit like Cinderella, but I know I would want Lydia home by then.'

'Yes, Auntie Jane,' answered Hannah, using the name she had called her by ever since pre-school days. 'I promise to be home by then. I think we are just going to walk along the harbour and see the boats lit up.'

'Hannah, you must do more than that,' Lydia's dad told her. 'You need to see the statue of Pythagoras – the town is named after him, the great Greek mathematician. You can't visit the town and not see the statue – take a photo on your phone to show Lydia. It's very famous!'

'I'll make sure Mike takes me there and I promise you a photo, Uncle John,' said Hannah with a smile. This was turning out to be a great day!

Nakato had been sleeping while all this chatting was going on, but she stirred and sat up in her bed. She looked tired and sad, but smiled at Lydia and her visitors.

'Hi, Nakato,' said Lydia, with a wave. 'These people are my mum, dad and my best friend, Hannah.'

Nakato smiled shyly and Lydia told them that she had come from Uganda. She knew that what Nakato had told her was very personal and private, so she didn't want to tell anyone the story of what had happened to her new friend without asking her permission first.

The bell rang loudly and it meant the hospital rules had to be obeyed yet again. Visiting time had ended – so Lydia hugged her parents and Hannah and whispered in Hannah's ear to remind her about holiday romances. Hannah giggled, blushed and whispered back, 'Don't put anything on Instagram, promise?'

'I haven't got my phone with me – the doc thinks it might trigger another fit,' she answered, with a grin. 'But just you wait until I get it back!'

When the ward was quiet again, Nakato got out of bed and went to get herself sorted, because of the 'LUL' problem, as the girls had decided to call it. 'LUL' was their shorthand for 'Leaky Urine, Loo'). Somehow, making a joke out of it helped Nakato to feel accepted and not an outcast. She could even giggle when she needed LUL. Then she came back and sat next to Lydia.

'Your parents are so kind. I can see they love you, and your friend, too. I always longed to have parents who really loved me – but I do have Musome.'

'Yes, you do,' answered Lydia. 'Can you tell me some more of your story? How did you actually escape?'

Chapter fourteen

'Almost at the end of the university term, Musome came to visit me. He had borrowed a camera and took some photos of my face, then told me he was getting me some legal papers. Once they were ready, then he promised to come for me. He told me to be ready, and to tie my spare clothes in a cloth and hide them in the *shamba*. It was dry season and so I had no problem with that. I did leave my work in the *shamba* one day very soon after Musome's visit, and ran all the way to the place of burial and knelt at my baby's grave. I picked a few wild flowers and laid them there. I asked Allah and Jesus to take care of him, not knowing who was the real, or the most powerful, God.

'One morning as I was working, hoeing the weeds around the cassava, I heard my name being called and there was my brother and two friends. I was frightened at the sight of the men and hid myself. Musome told me not to be afraid.

'"Nakato," he told me, "we are here to help you escape. Don't be afraid of my friends. Go and put on your headscarf in the Moslem fashion, collect your bundle and come. We have a long way to walk today, before anyone discovers you have gone."

'We walked together, my face hidden by my scarf and Musome's arm around me, protecting me, and I left Kapenguria forever.

'We walked and walked until evening came and it was dark, saying very little to each other, then went into the bush to find a place to sleep. The boys had brought food and water for us all, so that first night we did not make a fire or cook. We were so tired and all I wanted to do was to sleep, but Musome wanted me to meet his two friends properly, and talk with them. He wanted to reassure me that there was no reason to be scared. I could trust them, they were good people, who only wanted to help.

'Musome had papers for me – I promised to keep them safe. There was a Ugandan passport, which he put into a plastic bag, then into one made of bark cloth, and tied it with strips of bark cloth.

'"Tie this bag around your waist and do not show it to anyone until you know you are safe in Europe," he said to me. "It will get you safely to England, for inside is a letter to say that your mother's great-grandfather had been a soldier in the African Rifles and fought for the king of England."

'I had no idea that anyone in my family had fought for a king! Musome was sure the officials at the border for Britain would allow me to start a new life in England when they knew that. I hoped he was right.

'Then he also had other papers for me, to allow me to cross the border into Ethiopia. There was a letter for me to take to a hospital in Addis Ababa where an English doctor helps make girls like me with LUL get better. One of Musome's friends was studying to be a doctor and he had found out all about the operation I would need, and written the letter. There was money inside that letter to pay the hospital bills. I thanked him so much and for the first time since my baby had died, I felt a little hope. After the boys explained all this to me, they talked to their God, Jesus, and asked Him to take care of all of us. Then at last I could lay down and sleep.

'As dawn broke, we woke up.

'"Are you alright this morning, Nakato?" one of the young men asked me. I felt some of my shyness leave me.

'"I'm very stiff from lying on the cold ground," I answered. "I think we walked a long way yesterday."

'"We must start walking again, and we'll keep to the mud tracks, today, just in case anyone has come to search for you," he answered. "God will take care of us, don't be afraid."

'So, we started to walk again. At one place we found a stream. Musome guarded me so that I could wash and not smell so badly. The other two young men went to a nearby village to get supplies. Then we walked on and on until the sun set and the sky once again became dark. I don't know how many days we walked like this – the four of us together. Nobody bothered us. We even found we could go to the village stalls and markets and buy food, for by this time we were far from home. My feet were sore and bleeding, for I had no shoes, and in one village the boys bought me some flip-flops. I was so excited because I hadn't worn shoes since my wedding day. The walking was easier after that.'

'Did you reach Ethiopia?' asked Lydia.

Nakato shook her head. She began to cry softly.

'Don't tell me any more if you are getting upset,' said Lydia, gently.

'It's alright,' answered Nakato. 'I feel better for telling you my story, but things got worse once we reached the border with Ethiopia. The boys had to leave me there and go back to university. Musome had nearly finished his studies and then he hoped to get a good job and earn enough money to help all our family. Musome bought me two new smart dresses and some proper underwear, which I had never had before. He also bought me a bag to wear on my back, some food and gave me American dollars to help me on my way.

'"Put the dollars safely in the bark cloth bag with your passport," he told me. "I'm really sorry that we can only bring you this far. We want to pray for you now. Remember that Jesus will take care of you."

'The boys quietly and gently put their hands on my shoulders and asked their God, Jesus, to look after me. I felt very peaceful when they did that.

'Once they had left me, however, I felt very, very alone and fear came back. Because of the LUL, I had a job to keep myself clean and not to smell horrible. I found somewhere in the bush to sleep that night and in the morning got up to walk over the border. I had my papers with me, ready to show the guards. I had kept my other papers in the bark cloth bag around my waist just as I had promised Musome I would.

'The guards questioned me and I told them that I needed an operation in Addis Ababa. They put me in a small room, and I was frightened. Later, one of them told me to come, and so I followed him. He put in me in a truck but instead of driving me through the border post, he turned around and drove me many miles to the east – much later I learned he had kidnapped me and taken me to another country called Somalia.

'I was driven to a rebel army camp. I later found out that other people were also prisoners there. It seemed that they kidnapped many girls and young women. My papers to cross the border to Ethiopia, plus all the Kenyan Shillings my brother gave me, were taken from me, but they did not take my bark cloth bag which contained my passport, letter about my family and the American dollars. I think they thought it was a magic talisman given to me by the witchdoctor, so they were afraid to touch it. It did smell, too; I wasn't able to wash very often and – well, you know about the LUL. I think they thought it was rotten chicken guts – a favourite curse of witchdoctors. If only they had known what was really there!'

Nakato paused and chuckled to herself.

'There were all those important things hidden in it. Also, the rebel soldier who had kidnapped me hoped I would be a bride for one of his group – but when they tried to rape me they were disgusted by my condition, so left me alone. I was used as a slave around the camp. There were several young girls who had been kidnapped and they had a far worse time than I did; they were raped every day and those who were not Moslems were forced to change religion – at gunpoint. A few were so brave and refused – they said they were followers of the true God, Jesus. He must be a wonderful God, because they died, rather than give Him up. Often, they were raped and beaten before they were shot. It was done publicly, with all of us having to watch. It was so horrible to see, but we were forced to look.

'After a few weeks, that group of rebels decided they were going to raid a boat as pirates – and took me on their boat to cook for them. All my years cooking for my stepmother and then the other wives of my husband had given me experience in cooking well, and they liked my food. It was horrible on the boat – I felt sick many times, but still had to work. If I did not do well I was beaten. My back has many scars to show that.

'The day came when they attacked another boat. I lay in the bottom of our boat, covered by a tarpaulin, scared as bullets exploded everywhere. Then the boat was taken over by another group of men. They searched everywhere for loot, and discovered me. I thought I was going to be shot, but one of the men took pity on me and pleaded for my life to be saved. I was put into a small boat, then taken to a larger one. I had no idea who these men were and could not understand their language at all, but they were wearing Arab dress. When we arrived on the shore, the same man who saved me took me with him to his house.

'You can imagine how terrified I was – I had no idea what would happen next. However, he was a good man and his wife got water for me so that I could wash and she found me new clothes. I still wore my bark cloth bag, and had my Pokot necklaces – she didn't try to take them, but dressed me like an Arab lady in a burka. I thought that I would stay with her as her maid, but it was not to be, probably because I couldn't understand her language.

'After two days, she brought a man and a woman to see me. They spoke some English and asked me questions. I tried to answer carefully, for by now I didn't trust anybody. I had given up any thought of reaching Ethiopia, so when they asked where I was hoping to go, I said, England. They looked very surprised but promised to help me. They told me that it would be a very, very long journey to get north by sea to a country called Iran and then a very long walk to another country, Turkey – and from there I could get a boat to Europe.

'Why these people helped me I will never know, but they were like angels. They gave me clothes, warm clothes which I would need for travelling, a new bag for my back, with food, some Arabic money, although I had no idea how much it was worth, and a copy of the Koran. They informed me that if I had the Koran, then in Iran I would be safe for it would be seen that I was Moslem. I was in a country called Yemen – but I had no idea where that was until much later when someone showed me a map.

'I asked them how the sea journey would be paid for and was told that the fare had been purchased by the man who had rescued me, but once I reached Iran, I would have to look after myself and try to find a group of migrants who were travelling to Turkey and join them. It would be safer to travel in a large group.'

Chapter fifteen

'That night I was put on the boat. The sailors were polite to me – they seemed to respect the people who had helped me. I was very scared, yet thankful to be free and on my journey once again. I kept wondering about Musome and hoped he wouldn't worry about me. I wondered how long it would be before I reached Iran. I was given a small room below the deck and near the engines. It was noisy and smelly, but at least I was on my own – for a while. I hated the sea. I was scared. Many times I was sick and found it hard to eat the food served to me. It wasn't like the food I was used to eating. I longed for a plate of cassava and beans, such as I had grown in my garden.

'I cannot tell you how many days we were at sea – it seemed like forever. I got a fever and guessed I had malaria. I lay on the tiny bed in the room for many days, but the steward brought water for me to drink, and dry bread. I felt so ill that I wanted to die.

'We had sailed around the coast of a country called Oman and then the ship stopped at a port. At that place, another older lady came on board and was put into my room, which had two tiny beds on top of each other. I had to move to the top one because the older lady couldn't climb up. I felt terrible, I didn't want her to smell my clothes or bedding and now I had no privacy to take care of my LUL. We could not speak the same language, so it was hard for both of us. I tried to learn a little, so that we could be friends.

'One day I was walking up on the deck to get some fresh air when I heard a sailor call out – land had been sighted. "Iran!" he shouted – so I knew that we had arrived and soon I would be on land.'

The Greek nurse smiled to herself as she saw the two girls deep in conversation. She was so pleased, because no one had been able to get the deeply traumatised African girl to speak. She walked over to them and told them, with many gestures, that it was time to eat. Neither of them were used to Greek food, and hospital food everywhere is not the most appetising, but they did their best. When they were given bowls of thick yoghurt with honey for their dessert, broad smiles came over both girls – that was something they both liked.

As they were finishing this, the ward door opened, and in walked Dave. He had come to find out how the young girl he had rescued was getting on, and hoped he might be allowed to see Lydia, too, but was amazed to find them together and obviously becoming good friends.

'Dave,' said Lydia. 'How fantastic to see you!'

'Hey there, Lydia,' he greeted her. 'I have been allowed in – even against the rules – because I need to see this young lady whom I rescued from the sea, and the nurse said I could visit you, too. I heard that you're much better – and I can see you've made friends!'

'You're the one who saved Nakato – that's really cool! I know you work with refugees. Please will you take care of her? She has had such terrible experiences. We have been talking – she speaks amazing English, but neither of us can speak Greek, so we've been saved from a terrible silent recovery!'

'Dave,' said Nakato. 'You were the man who came into the horrible cold sea and saved me? How can I say enough times to you, thank you! I would have drowned if you hadn't come. But baby Ali – what about Ali? I asked about him many times, here in the hospital and nobody understands or tells me.'

Dave sat next to Nakato and took her hand. He had tears in his eyes and told her that when he had rescued her, she was clutching the baby and would not let him go, but Ali was already dead. Nothing they could do would bring him back to life; indeed, they thought at first that she would die as well.

Nakato began to cry, huge heart-rending sobs. Lydia put her arms around her friend – she didn't know anything about a baby but could see the pain she was feeling. Dave was weeping, too, and neither of them said anything. What could they say to comfort her?

After a while Nakato quietened. 'What happened to his body?' she asked.

'The doctor and nurses on the cruise ship wrapped him carefully in clean sheets and a little body bag, and the chaplain buried him in the sea with a short service, committing him to God. One of the nurses had tied a bunch of flowers and threw them where his body had been buried,' Dave gently explained. 'It is what happens when someone dies at sea.'

'Thank you for telling me. I really loved little Ali and had promised to take care of him, but there was no life jacket for him – there was no chance to save him.' Tears welled up again in Nakato's eyes. 'I'll never forget that terrible night; those men who took all our money, then squashed us into a small boat – pushed us out with poles that made holes in its sides, and allowed us to capsize without helping. It was terrible, so terrible and so wicked!'

Dave was concerned at Nakato's distress and went to find the nursing sister on duty. He could speak a little Greek and managed to get her to understand. Nakato was given an injection to help her calm down and go to sleep.

'Tomorrow when she wakes, I know you will be there for her. All the memories will come back – she will need a good friend. How wonderful that you have the bed next to her and she can speak English. I was so upset to hear about your fit, but perhaps there was a reason – so that you could be here to help Nakato,' said Dave.

Lydia nodded. 'Can I tell you something? The only person I have shared this with is Hannah. I know that when I was unconscious after the hit-and-run accident, I was in a place of wonderful light and I wanted to stay and rest there, but heard a voice tell me it wasn't time yet, there were things for me to do on the earth. I think it was God. I didn't really believe in God before, but I do now. Maybe this is one of those things God wants me to do, to listen to Nakato.

'She's been telling me her story – and she has had a terrible life. I don't know all of it yet, but hope I can learn the rest before I get back to the hotel tomorrow. I want to be able to help her and need to speak to Dad about that, but he's gone back to the ship – it had to sail on to the next port of call.'

'Don't worry. We won't abandon Nakato. We'll do our best to make sure she gets to a place of safety,' promised Dave. 'It's getting late. I'd better go. I'd love to stay with you and talk for longer, but the nurse broke the rules and let me in, so I mustn't take advantage. Hey, thanks for sharing what happened to you after the accident. I think that's great – you heard God speak to you. Lately, things have been making me think about Him, too. I don't know much, but want to learn more. By the way, Lydia, I love your hair short – it's spunky, like you are.'

'Oh, thanks, that's really nice of you to say. I lost my wig in the storm when I had that fit. It was a bit hot to wear, but I wasn't sure if I would look a freak without it.'

'A freak!' answered Dave. 'You are beautiful – it just shines from you – never let anyone tell you otherwise.'

Lydia was touched, almost embarrassed by Dave's reply. Her mind flitted back to Sam's reaction when he had seen her in hospital in London. He hadn't been able to see beyond the scars that she was just the same girl inside. Dave's words made her feel warm and glowing. Was she falling for Dave? That thought made her think of Hannah.

'Just one thing before you leave, Dave,' she said a bit hesitantly. 'I really hate to ask you, but I'm a bit worried about Hannah. She's badly smitten with your brother. She's got a date with him tonight – they're going to

111

Pythagoreio. Mum said she could go, but asked her to be back by midnight. I know he's your brother, but he will take care of her, won't he? We've not really had boyfriends – I was starting to date a boy from school, who had been my escort to the school prom, and I thought was gorgeous, but after I had the accident he didn't want to know me any more – who could blame him? My face is scarred for life, but I realise now he was shallow inside and just wanted a good time. I'm just a bit afraid for Hannah.'

Dave looked concerned. 'Don't worry, Lydia, I'll make sure she's OK. I know the bar in Pythagoreio he likes to visit. I'll go there on my way home right now. He does flirt a bit with the female guests, but he means no harm, and I'm sure he wouldn't take advantage of Hannah in any way.'

Dave gave Lydia a hug and left her to get a good sleep. She felt so much better having told him her worries. The hug made her feel comforted and she snuggled down, thinking what a great guy he was.

Dave was a bit worried. He knew his twin brother liked having a girl on his arm and could be a terrible flirt, never bothering to think the girls might get hurt when he tired of them and found someone else. Hannah was younger than most of the girls Mike had taken out, and so sweet, too. He didn't want her to get hurt, but he had noticed the attraction between the two of them. Mike hadn't said anything to him, but Dave sensed that he did care about Hannah.

He took a taxi rather than wait for the bus, so that he could reach Pythagoreio more quickly. He walked down the narrow street which led to the harbour. All the shops were open and the little town was buzzing with life. It was a lovely place to visit on a warm autumn evening. All along the harbour were cafés, restaurants and bars. Even though it was late in the season, there still seemed to be a good number of tourists around. As Dave walked along he glanced at the couples walking hand in hand. He guessed that Mike would have taken Hannah to see the boats, many of which were lit up and looked very pretty in the evening. At the end of the harbour, not far from the old castle, was the café bar he knew Mike liked and where he often went on his evenings off.

As Dave walked there, he wondered how Mike and Hannah would receive him. He didn't want to wrongly judge his brother, but neither did he want Hannah to get hurt, and he had promised Lydia he would go and find them. He guessed Mike would not be at all happy to see him.

When he reached the café, his brother was at the bar getting drinks. He was glad to see that Hannah had ordered a cola. He slapped his twin on the back and jovially said to him, 'Hey, bro, get me a lemonade while you're at it!'

Mike swung around, anger showing in his face. 'What are you doing here? I thought you were working with your refugees tonight. Have you come to spoil my date?'

'I have been with them. Well, with one of them – the girl I pulled out of the sea in the storm. She was so upset when she heard that baby she was clutching was dead, I couldn't face doing anything more this evening,' Dave told Mike.

Mike's anger disappeared as quickly as it had come. He really admired his brother for all the work he did to help other people, even though he teased him about it. How sad that a baby had died. Mike loved children, and the thought of one drowning because of the greed of people traffickers disgusted him.

'Sure, I'll get you a drink. Don't you want anything stronger after that ordeal?' he asked.

'No, thanks, I'm hot and thirsty. I wouldn't mind an ice cream, though,' Dave answered.

'Good idea. Hannah's over there, looking out to sea – ask her if she'd like an ice cream and which flavour she fancies.'

Dave walked over to Hannah, sighing with relief that Mike wasn't angry with him. As he approached, Hannah smiled. She liked Dave, although he didn't attract her in the way Mike did. She was glad he had turned up because although she had enjoyed the walk and visiting the statue of Pythagoras with Mike holding her hand, she had felt a little scared when he had tried to kiss her – a real kiss, not a peck on the cheek or a brush over her lips. It had excited her and stirred her, but she had been scared by her reaction. She wasn't sure she was ready for such intimacy yet and had pushed him away. Thank goodness he had got the message and didn't seem cross with her, but had smiled at her with his gorgeous smile that made her insides melt.

The three of them had fun together, just chatting, eating fabulous ice creams and sipping their drinks.

'Could we come here again as a foursome when Lydia is out of hospital?' Hannah asked the boys. 'I feel so mean having fun while she has had so little. This holiday was to give her a break and happier things to think about, but it hasn't worked out exactly as we planned.'

'Hey, that's a great idea,' answered Dave. 'I can push her in the wheelchair. Will her mum mind being left alone for one evening if Captain John is still on his ship?'

'I think she'll just be pleased for Lydia to have some fun – it's been months since she's had a normal life. Auntie Jane is used to being on her own quite a lot, because Uncle John is away at sea.'

The three of them walked back along the harbour, enjoying the warm evening, and then caught a taxi back to the hotel. Mike saw Hannah to her room, and gave her a quick hug and a kiss on the cheek, thanking her for the evening.

'See you tomorrow, Hannah – sleep tight, and may all your dreams be of me,' he said.

'Cheeky!' she retorted. 'Only if your dreams are all of me.'

For a few moments Mike was silent, then spoke softly to her. 'They will be – you are really special to me, Hannah. One day, when you 're ready, I'll give you that real kiss. Forgive me for trying earlier. I didn't mean to scare you; I just find you irresistible,' and then he disappeared down the corridor.

Dave was waiting for him on the hotel terrace.

'She really is a bit young for you, twino,' he commented, 'but you do seem to like her a lot.'

'I know,' Mike told his brother. 'She's only sixteen and yet something about her innocence and sweetness really gets me. You know, she wouldn't even let me kiss her properly – yet I'm glad she didn't. I admire her for that. I feel I want to protect her, but not in a big brotherly way. I've never felt like this before with a girl; usually I just like to have a fun time and when they go home I don't feel anything. I'm already dreading the fact that Hannah will soon go back to Croydon and college and I might not see her again for a long time. She'll probably have loads of boys her age asking her out and I don't really know how she feels about me.'

'Hey, bro, you really are smitten by her,' remarked Dave. 'Actually, Lydia is a remarkable young lady, too – so mature and understanding that I forget she's only sixteen. I wouldn't say that I'm smitten, but I feel very drawn to her, and she's so beautiful in spite of all her facial scars. We'll have to be very careful not to hurt these two girls. I think they're both vulnerable in their own way.'

'You're right as usual, big bro, even if you are only half an hour older than me,' Mike said with a grin, 'and I was stupid to even try to kiss Hannah in the way I did. It will be cool to have a foursome date together.'

Chapter sixteen

The next morning Lydia was longing to hear the rest of Nakato's story. She wondered who baby Ali was – had Nakato given birth to another child on the journey? Surely she had said she could not have any more children? Her curiosity had to wait because that morning she was scheduled to be wired up to a machine and have her brainwaves read. Lydia was no longer scared by the procedure, for she had had EEGs performed several times in the hospital after her accident. It was just more difficult when so few of the hospital staff were able to speak any English. She was longing to get out and return to the hotel and enjoy the rest of the holiday, but felt sad that she would leave her new friend on her own.

Once the EEG had been performed, Lydia was wheeled back into the ward just as mid- morning drinks were being served. Nakato was waiting for her – her chair already near the window where they had sat yesterday. Having been sedated the night before, Nakato had slept late, but she did seem happier and wanted to continue telling Lydia her story.

'So, what happened when you reached Iran?' asked Lydia.

'Well, I realised that I had a problem. I didn't want to reveal my passport and money – I knew I would need that at a later point in my journey – but I had to get off the ship and on to the land. I had packed my few things in the backpack and helped the older woman, who was called Fatou, to get ready. By now I had learned a few words of Arabic from her and the steward and found that several words were almost the same as Swahili, which I knew from living in Kenya. She indicated that I should stay and help her with her case and I was glad to do that. Fatou walked with a stick and one hand was deformed. We walked together quite slowly down the gangplank, where she was met by two large young men. I gave her case to one of them, but she grabbed my hand, spoke softly and quickly to the men, and we were all hustled out, waved through the controls and put into a large Mercedes car and driven away. By now I was scared – was I being kidnapped again?

'Fatou kept hold of my hand and smiled, telling me not to worry – at least I think that's what she said. We arrived at a large house with fancy railings and gates. Once more I felt scared – was it a prison? Could I ever escape through those gates?

'Fatou was welcomed by lots of people in the house. Then a young lady spoke to me, but I shook my head as I couldn't understand – she was speaking very quickly. Then she tried again in another language – she must have been very clever, for finally she tried in English.

'"You are welcome here. Grandmother Fatou has told us how kind you have been and how much you have helped her. She was the *ayah* – nanny – for this family, but now is old and lives with us, although she once was our servant. She has been away visiting her relatives. Come in and have some tea with us."

'I was so glad to be able to talk in English, but still very afraid of trusting anyone with my story. The young lady was a daughter of the household. Her name was Ayisha, and she could see I was scared. We had tea and she asked if I would be their guest for a while. Then I explained that I had been on my way to Ethiopia for an operation when I was kidnapped and my papers and money were stolen. Now I needed to get to Europe and hopefully to England. Ayisha told me that I was in a town called Shiraz, a long way from the border with Turkey, but she knew that there were many migrants from Syria fleeing from war who were travelling through the country. She explained to me that I would be safer travelling with a group. She asked me to stay a few days while she found out the best way for me to continue.

'"Our family are influential and we have many contacts. Trust me, I will get help for you," she told me.

'I began to trust Ayisha, and told her about my LUL; I did not want to embarrass this rich family. I explained about the operation my brother had arranged and that I was an outcast until it was done.

'"You poor girl," she said. "Don't worry. I will try to help. I see you are a good Moslem, keep wearing your burka and pray to Allah for help. No one will molest you here, you are safe."

'I stayed with Grandmother Fatou in her room for two days, and kept very quiet. I was scared. I did pray when the call came from the mosque – but to Jesus, because I felt if any God could help me, it would be Him.

'Ayisha did as she promised, and was so kind to me. Her brothers knew important people and they made some new papers for me, so that I could cross into Turkey. Then she gave me some nice clothes, for we were about the same size, and Iranian money and bars of dried fruit and sweets which would go in my backpack. After staying in their house for a few days, late one night, I said goodbye to Fatou, and under the cover of darkness, Ayisha's oldest brother drove me in the big car for a long way. The dawn was breaking when we arrived at a makeshift refugee camp. He registered me, and talked for a long time to the man in charge. Then he said goodbye, told me that I would be looked after, and drove away. I had little time even to give him my thanks.

'I was taken to a large group of refugees who were about to set off on the long walk to Turkey. I was told to stay with the group, and one large family were asked to take care of me. They were not from Syria, but from Pakistan and could speak English. It was a relief – but still I was scared. I huddled into my burka, glad that I was hidden except for my eyes.

'We began our walk that very day. It took days and weeks and months, walking in the coolest part of the day and camping in the countryside at night. I learned to read the stars – they were so beautiful. The family I was travelling with were kind to me and gradually I became less afraid and spoke more. The mother had six young children, and I helped her with them, especially the baby, Ali. I cried less for my own little baby as I cuddled and played with Ali. That family shared their food with me, and I shared the little I had, and pooled the money which I had been given. I had no idea how much it was, but we always managed to have a little to eat and a hot drink of tea.

'When the rains started, life became much more difficult. We were cold and wet and trudging through thick mud. Many of the migrants on the road became sick with dysentery and some died on the way. The men dug shallow graves and we tried to give them a decent burial. We eventually came near to the border with Turkey, and the Pakistani family I was travelling with told me to stay close and they would help me through the border. It seemed that papers were not enough – the border officials wanted money, too. The amount Ayisha had given me must have been quite a lot, because we were admitted. I sighed with relief – this was the last country to travel across before we would catch a boat to Europe.

'We just kept walking and walking, every day the same. Ali's mother grew sick, and one horrible day she died. We buried her beside the road. All of us were so sad, but we had to keep going. I took over the care of all the six children, as best as I could. The father and his brother still protected me and I was treated as family, in spite of all my LUL problems. After a while I shared a little of my story with them – they had proved trustworthy and deserved to know who I really was. In turn, they trusted me with their story. Like my brother Musome, they had been brought up as Moslems, but then they learned about the Jesus God and wanted to follow Him. When people in their country learned that they had become Christians, they were hated and persecuted. The family received many death threats, so they knew, especially for the sake of the children, they had to flee. For months they saved all the money they could and then began to make the journey to safety and a new life.

'"We still travel as Moslems," they told me. "It is safer, for we travel through Moslem countries. Please keep our secret for the safety of the children."

'I promised to do so and to help this kind family as much as I could. I could never take the place of their sweet mother, but I could be much kinder to them than my stepmothers were to me.'

Nakato had to stop telling her story because the doctors were arriving to see their patients. They returned to their beds. Lydia's doctor was pleased with her.

'The brain tracing is good. Tonight I will allow your mother to take you away. I have to plan your drugs and have them ready so you stay until evening,' he told her in broken English. Lydia beamed. She was very happy – but what about her friend, Nakato?

Nakato had a different doctor looking after her who didn't seem to speak English, but he seemed very pleased with her improvement.

They ate their lunch together and Lydia knew she would not have long to hear the rest of the story. For once, the hospital rules must be broken, she decided. When it was the rest hour before visitors, she and Nakato would whisper to each other while they lay on their beds.

Chapter seventeen

Lydia had been glad to hear that there were at least some kind people who had helped Nakato on her way – but the end of the story was not so good.

'After weeks of travelling we arrived at a city called Izmir,' Nakato told her. 'Some of the group of migrants from Syria had relatives already staying there, others had money to rent an apartment and they even began small businesses in the streets while they negotiated getting places on a boat to Europe. There are men called people traffickers who charge very high prices and fix up the transport. They make lots of money out of the poor, desperate migrants who will pay anything to get to Europe and start a new life. They are horrible men.

'First you must find a go-between man and he will arrange a meeting with a trafficker. Much of this is done in secret because it is illegal, although the police know about it and do nothing. Khamran, the father of the children I was looking after, began to try to buy passages for us. The police picked him up and tried to force him to stay in

Turkey and be a soldier. They promised he would be safe doing that. Khamran refused to join the army, so then his brother had to be the next one to have a secret meeting to buy the passages. I was sent with him along with baby Ali, as they thought that might be the best way to do it. They prayed to Jesus first.

'I was dressed in my burka and shrank away from looking at the man we were meeting, but he kept looking at me. He asked many questions and when he found out that I was not the wife, he wanted me to take off my burka so that he could see what I really looked like. I was horrified and scared – I remembered Somalia when they had tried to rape me.

'I was taken to a small room and Ali was given to his uncle to hold. The man told me I was beautiful and he would buy me nice European clothes to wear and take me to good places and find me a good job in England. Why didn't I leave these Pakistani people and stay with him? He would take me to England and I would have a good life. If I did what he said, he told me my worries would all be over. He was very persuasive and I was very scared. It seemed an easy way to get to England, but other migrants had warned me of these people who took young women and made them sex slaves in other countries.

'I hated doing it, but I knew there was only one way to escape this, for he was ready to take me by force if I did not go willingly with him. I had to expose myself and show him where I had been cut and torn and leaked all the time. I felt such shame – so dirty and so horrible. He took one look at me and growled in anger, "Get your clothes on and get out of here!"

'Khamran's brother was surprised to see me – he thought I had been kidnapped. Ali cried and held out his arms to me and I took and cuddled him.

'"A boat sails to Samos tomorrow night," the man said, handing a piece of paper over. "If you can find 10,000 American dollars by then, this is where you have to hand over the money and get your tickets."

'We left the house where we had met the horrible man, and almost ran through the back streets to the place where we were living rough. Neither of us spoke – indeed, we were out of breath. Khamran and the other children were waiting for us – hopeful when we rushed in. We sat down on the floor and I burst into tears. What could we do – how could we get so much foreign money?

'I listened as Khamran heard the story from his brother. I felt too ashamed to tell them what I had done. Obviously by now they knew I had some problems and needed an operation, but I could not bring myself to tell them what the man had suggested and how had I escaped.

'The amount asked was just too much. I was surprised because the two men just talked to their God, Jesus, and asked Him to provide it. Then, suddenly, I remembered I did have some American dollars for my journey. I had carefully guarded them all this time, ready to pay for my own fare – but I had no idea how many were in the bark cloth bag I still wore around my waist. I was sure that my brother would not have been able to earn or save very much.

'I excused myself and went to the toilet where I could have a little privacy. I took off my bark cloth bag and took out the money, leaving just the passport and letters inside the plastic bag, which I sealed again.

'I took it to Khamran and told him this was what my brother had given me for my journey to Europe. He had told me it was American money. The money was wrapped in paper, on which was writing. While Khamran counted the dollars, I read the letter. It was written in the Pokot language and I had tears streaming down my face as I read it out loud – just to hear my own language again was amazing. So were the things written in the letter. It went something like this:

My dear sister Nakato,

This money is for you to get to Europe. We prayed and asked God how much you would need and he told us $10,000. It seemed so much, but we didn't argue with God, but set about working to raise the money – not just me and my close friends, but all the Christians in the university. Some ran long distances and told your story and people gave money, others worked extra hours to get money for you, others asked their churches to give – and when we counted it up and went to the forex bureau to change it into American dollars, we were given exactly $10,000! This miracle changed my heart, I am now openly a follower of Jesus, and have asked for baptism. We give it to you with joy, so that you will know that Jesus loves you, too. When you reach England (and I know you will), write to me at

Makerere University, Kampala, so that all of us can
share your joy.

Your beloved brother,
Musome

'As I read out this letter and translated it, the men began to cry. They praised their God and blessed Him. Then Khamran paused, and said to me, "This is your money, Nakato. You must go to safety."

'I knew at once this money was not meant only for me.

'"Why would your God give me all this money when it is exactly the amount asked for all of us to go to safety?" I asked him. "I will not go without you all. I would not have got to this place without your help and kindness – we will pay the money and go together!"

'After a while they realised that I meant what I said, so they agreed. Next day the money was paid and the seats on the boat bought. We were told where to be as soon as it became dark and we would be taken by truck to the shore.

'It all happened just as we were told. We were squashed into the back of the truck – so many of us I could not count them all. Once we reached the beach, we were put into small rubber boats and only a few of us had life jackets to wear, so that we would float if we were shipwrecked. Khamran insisted I had one, and Ali was on my lap. There were far too many people on the boat and we were pushed out from the shore by long poles. These pierced the sides and water soon began to come in. We could see how close this island was, so the men rowed, and all who could tried to scoop the seawater out of the boat. Then the storm began, and with the thunder and lightning we were even more terrified.

'The boat capsized and we were thrown into the cold, black sea. I was trying to hold Ali up – I think I knew he was going to die. There were many terrible screams which still keep ringing in my ears, especially when I try to sleep at night. I thought I might die, too, but suddenly, someone lifted me up, and the next thing I remember was lying here in this hospital. Now I know it was that kind man, Dave, who saved me, and that Ali did die. I keep wondering about the rest of the family – did they all die, too? Why would this God Jesus give money for us all to escape if everybody else died? Was it the anger of Allah? I am very confused.'

Nakato became distressed and Lydia didn't know how to comfort her. She was cross with herself – she had been so selfish wanting to hear the end of the story.

'I'm so sorry,' Lydia kept telling Nakato. 'I shouldn't have pressed you to tell me the rest of the story. Please forgive me. I'm truly sorry.'

Nakato dried her eyes and sniffed. 'It's not your fault. I wanted you to know it all. I don't understand why it has all happened like this and I don't know what to do next. I'm still a long, long way from England and all my money has gone, and maybe my friends.'

The ward sister had seen the girls talking, but had decided to turn a blind eye and let them disobey the rules. It was good for the Ugandan girl to talk and the British girl would go home that evening. Sister was worried about who would help the Ugandan girl – she had asked for the refugee liaison officer to visit, but she had not come yet.

Perhaps she was having trouble getting a translator to help her.

Visiting time arrived, and as Nakato was awake, Lydia was able to introduce her properly to her parents and Hannah. Lydia hadn't expected to see her dad, but having taken his ship to the next port of call, a helicopter had brought him back to Samos so that he could stay with them for the last few days of the holiday. Lydia's mum packed her belongings into a bag, so that they could leave as soon as the drugs were ready.

'Mum,' said Lydia. 'Please leave all my toiletries and the nice, soft towel for Nakato. She has nothing of her own.'

'Of course, dear, what a good idea. I'll pop out to the shops and buy her some other bits and pieces, while we wait for your drugs,' Jane suggested.

With Nakato's permission, Lydia told her dad and Hannah just a little of what her new friend had endured and how worried she was about her future. John was very interested and asked Nakato quite a lot of questions, especially about the man who was trafficking people from Turkey to Samos and taking their money, their mobile phones (if they had them), even their passports, but hers had been safely hidden in the bag. Nakato was able to describe the man very well because she had been alone with him in the small room.

'The first thing I noticed was his right arm,' she told John. 'He had a huge snake tattooed on it, which curled round his arm. It looked like a cobra to me. He also had a scar over his left eyebrow – a long one which was very noticeable. His nose was long and his black hair was greasy.

He had lots of gold chains around his neck and a huge watch on his right wrist.'

John was listening intently, and he recorded all that Nakato told him on a small device.

'Lydia tells me, Nakato, that you still have your passport and some letters that say that your mother's great-grandfather fought for Britain in the King's African Rifles in the Second World War. That is very good news. I have friends who, if you will let me tell them, might be able to help you to get a visa to come to England, firstly for medical help, and then as a refugee. Will you allow me to make enquiries tonight? I will try to get you transferred from the hospital into the refugee camp here in Samos town, while I make further arrangements to get you to England. I will do my very best for you.'

Nakato was so relieved. Jesus must have heard her prayers. Perhaps things would work out for her in the end.

'Thank you so much for trying to help me,' she said, tearfully.

Lydia said goodbye to Nakato, but promised she would visit her again, either in the hospital or the refugee camp, before they flew back to England. 'Don't worry any more – my dad is wonderful. He'll work something out, I'm sure. I'll pray to Jesus, too, for you to get safely to England.'

Chapter eighteen

'It's so good to be out of hospital and back at the hotel. At least I've only missed a few days of the holiday,' Lydia said, as the taxi drove into the hotel compound.

At dinner, all the sports team who were on duty came over to chat and welcome her back. The after-dinner entertainment was a quiz and the twins asked if she and Hannah would join their team. Lydia was thrilled because it was something she could do, even though both legs were in plaster. It proved to be great fun, especially as their team won by a huge margin, and they were all given silly sunglasses as prizes. Then her dad took a photo of them wearing them. She put it on Instagram to show her friends and got loads of 'likes' within minutes. When they weren't looking, she took a photo of Mike and Hannah who were sitting very close to each other and laughing over something. She was sure that Hannah would be pleased. She planned to get a frame for it and give it to her as a present.

Dave was sitting next to her and they chatted after the quiz.

'Hey, Lydia, how is Nakato?' he asked. 'It was so good that she was in the next bed and you could talk to each other in English.'

Lydia told him that her father was hoping to help Nakato get to England for an operation. Dave was pleased to hear that news and excused himself so that he could talk to John about it.

'I wanted a chat with you too, Dave,' Lydia's dad said. 'Pull up a chair and we can talk about Nakato. I understand from the girls that you help with the migrants in the refugee camp. I know that Lydia will not have told you much, but as well as my work as captain of the cruise ship I also do other investigative journalistic work for a newspaper, from time to time. At the moment, I'm investigating some of the issues around people trafficking and the abduction of young girls into the sex trade. What Nakato has told Lydia, and then me, is important evidence. When Nakato is discharged from hospital, I need her to be in a "safe" place – not just to be interviewed by the authorities here and issued with a "white paper" to go on to mainland Greece. Is there any way we can guarantee that? If not, I will have to persuade the hospital to keep her as an inpatient for a while.'

'There is one house – a place where some of the migrants who have their papers can live until they are moved on. It belongs to an Englishwoman, Pam, who works part-time in the office here and is married to a Greek – they want to give dignity to these poor people. In fact, the Pakistani family that Nakato has been with since she left

132

Iran are likely to go there, as they speak English well, but do not know Greek. I'll text Pam if you like and see if she is free to come over and have a meeting with us. She is utterly trustworthy and very compassionate.'

That evening, not only was the meeting arranged, with Pam promising to take care of Nakato until she could fly to England, but also John was able to contact his superior at the newspaper and because of the situation and Nakato's vulnerability, promised to set in motion the procedures to try to bring her to the UK on emergency medical grounds.

While all this was taking place, Hannah and Mike went for a late-night swim, and Lydia and her mum watched them from the shore, under the twinkling stars. Hannah was pleased they were there – she remembered the advice her mum had given her about dating when she had first started at high school that it was always better not to be alone with your date at the start of a relationship; you could both get carried away by your feelings and emotions and go further than you really wanted.

The next day Lydia got up early, and with Hannah's help she went to see the sun rise over the bay. It was glorious! As she looked out to the coast of Turkey, everywhere looked so calm and peaceful, it was difficult to imagine the stormy sea that night when she had had the fit. She thought how Nakato had almost drowned, and how Ali and many others had perished.

Her father had told her as she went to bed the previous evening that he would be leaving very early in the morning on business, to try to help Nakato, but would be back in the evening in time for dinner.

'I'm going over to Turkey on the early morning ferry. I shall be hungry when I get back so I hope there'll be plenty of food left for me!' he joked.

Lydia wanted to make the very most of the day, having missed some of the holiday. Dave had promised her a treat. Even though her legs were still in plaster, he was going to take her sailing.

'Hey, Lydia,' he said. 'Don't look so worried. I've been planning it while you were in the hospital. It'll be just great.'

He wheeled her to the beach and then sealed both of her legs in very strong polythene bags, so that the plaster wouldn't get wet, then lifted her up as if she weighed almost nothing, and carried her to the dinghy. One of the girls from the sports team was there to help him crew, and they sailed right around the bay. Lydia felt exhilarated – no wonder Hannah had loved learning to sail. Hannah and Mike were also on the water, but Hannah was taking her first test to see if she could get the beginner's certificate. The next day a regatta was planned and Hannah so wanted to take part in it. It was a chance for all the guests who had been sailing to show their skills and have great fun.

'Almost everyone wins a certificate of some sort. We have presentation evening, which is hilarious. You'll really enjoy it, Hannah, and you should receive your sailing certificate then,' Mike had told her.

After all the fun of sailing, Dave carefully carried Lydia back to her mother, who was sunbathing on the beach.

'That was great, taking you out on the sea,' Dave told her. 'Your holiday is speeding by, so we must make every minute count. I want you to go home looking suntanned.'

As her father was away for the day, Lydia had decided that she would stay with her mum through the afternoon. Hannah had also decided to stay with them. They enjoyed themselves playing with the giant Connect Four in the garden, sipping iced tea, and then reading under the shade of the palm trees which were dotted around the swimming pool. The twins had already arranged to take the girls to Pythagoreio for the evening, so they were glad to take things easy and relax in the sun, which was still warm, although it was early autumn.

'How do I look?' Hannah asked Lydia, when they were in their room changing for the evening. 'I want to look my best for Mike. Should I wear my white or my red top?'

'I think the white one will show off your tan best,' Lydia replied. 'Shall we do each other's make-up like we did for the prom? You really made my eyes up beautifully – and I have to make the most of what wasn't scarred by the accident,' she added, pushing her hand through her short hair.

'Great idea. I could do with a manicure, too, if there's time,' answered Hannah.

Lydia wished she could wear her jeans with her new sparkly top, but until the plaster casts were removed she had no choice but to wear skirts. She chose a long gypsy skirt which her mum had bought her for the holiday. It did look nice with the black, sparkly top.

The boys were treating them to dinner in an Italian restaurant – and they were pleased to think they could choose a pizza for a change. Lydia had her crutches, but also Dave folded up her wheelchair and put it in the boot of the taxi he had ordered. He told her it was quite a long walk around the harbour and he would love to push her.

'Hey, Lydia,' he said, with a laugh. 'It might be my very last chance to push you – once you get home you'll have the casts off. I need to get my practice in before I start to train as a medic, and who could be nicer to practise with then my beautiful new friend!'

Lydia blushed a little, and happily allowed herself to be pushed in the wheelchair. 'Isn't this fun,' she said to Hannah and the twins, 'wandering around the little shops?' The shops stayed open all the evening, and she wanted to buy her gran and gramps something special from Samos. After much deliberation, she bought them a piece of pottery – beautiful turquoise blue like the colour of the sea. It was an Archimedes cup. Inside was a device. If the cup was filled beyond that then all the liquid drained away – supposedly to stop people from drinking too much wine. It was unusual and she knew her grandparents would enjoy it. Turquoise was Gran's favourite colour.

The four of them walked along the waterfront. It was magical seeing all the boats lit up, many with fairy lights. Lydia took loads of photos on her phone, including the statue of Pythagoras to show her dad she had seen it with her own two eyes, as she wasn't convinced that Hannah had really seen it on her last visit, since she had eyes for no one but Mike! It seemed as if he was besotted with her, too.

They were in the middle of their meal when Lydia's phone rang. It was her mum. She was quite worried and although she didn't want to spoil the girls' evening, she felt that she ought to ask them to get home in good time because her father hadn't arrived back from his day in Turkey.

'He should have been back by now – the last ferry comes in before dark,' remarked Mike.

'I know Mum is worried, I can tell by the tone of her voice,' Lydia told the others. 'Would you mind if we went home as soon as we've finished eating?'

They ate the rest of their meals quickly and the boys called a taxi to take them back to the hotel. Dave was also worried, although he didn't say anything to Lydia. He had a gut feeling that John had gone over to Turkey to follow up the lead which Nakato had given him about the trafficker who had tried to abduct her. He could be in real danger. Those men cared for no one but themselves.

Once the girls were safely back at the hotel, Dave tried to reassure Jane, Lydia's mum. Then he said he would go and check on the ferries – maybe one was late returning. He asked Lydia to text him if they heard from her dad or if he returned to the hotel.

'Come on, twino,' he said, trying to sound cheerful. 'I could do with your company.'

They had asked the taxi to wait for them and then it took them into Samos town.

'What's going on?' questioned Mike, who had hoped for a romantic evening with Hannah. 'He's a grown man, quite capable of looking after himself!'

'He may be in trouble. I'm not sure what's going on, but as well as being a cruise ship captain, he does undercover investigative journalism for a newspaper,' Dave told his brother very quietly – aware that the taxi driver might hear and could possibly understand English.

'You mean he's a spy!' said Mike.

'Something like that – be careful Mike, little ears may be listening!' Dave commented, using a phrase their parents had used in their childhood. Mike got the message and stopped asking questions.

The taxi dropped them at a house in the centre of the town. It was where the Englishwoman, Pam, lived, and next door was the 'halfway house' where the Pakistani family had been installed earlier that day. Dave needed to talk to Khamran about his contact with the people smugglers.

Khamran was very helpful. He gave all the information he had, including contact phone numbers – for although his phone had been taken from him, along with all his belongings before they made the crossing, he had an amazing memory, especially when it came to numbers.

Dave thanked everyone for their help, and Pam was able to tell him that Nakato would be discharged and be living in the same house the next day. He promised to tell Lydia so that she could come and visit.

'Now we have some sailing to do,' Dave told his brother.

'What do you mean?' said Mike.

'I mean, twino, that we're going over to the Turkish coast. Captain John may need some help. We'll take our largest dinghy and try to find out what's happened,' Dave told him.

They found another taxi in the main square and were taken back to the hotel. The twins gathered some waterproof jackets and trousers, for the temperature had fallen considerably. They left a note for the team leader saying they were taking the largest dinghy on a mercy mission.

'The man whom the migrants have nicknamed "Cobra" – Captain John told me he's working to get him arrested – is the head of the people trafficking outfit over there. It's my opinion that the Turkish patrol have turned a blind eye to his activities. It's like the Mafia over there, from all I've heard from the migrants,' commented Dave.

Although the sea was quiet, it took a while for them to sail around the coast and over the straight between Samos and Turkey, trying to avoid the patrol boats from both countries. They also knew that some poor migrants might well be trying to cross, too – but the night was young yet. How glad they were that it wasn't a full moon, and clouds kept flitting across the sky, blotting out the sliver of the moon which could be seen. Having spent the whole summer sailing in that part of the coast, although they had never sailed into the Turkish waters, they had a pretty good idea where they could land. They had no real plan, but knew enough of what went on with the people smugglers to know that John might be in very real danger. The network was not just local to that part of the Turkish coast, but was spread throughout Turkey, Libya and Egypt – people taking advantage of the refugees and migrants. It was a billion-dollar business and, like the drug cartels of South America, these men were rich, powerful and ruthless.

The boys sailed into a small cove which seemed deserted. They dropped the anchor and waded to the shore, then took a path which led them inland. With the aid of maps, compass and torches, they set off to try to find the nearby cove which was used most evenings by the people smugglers. They knew that the migrants were transported there in trucks, and the thought was that they might be able to get a ride to the town in one of the trucks. It seemed a huge adventure, but very scary, too.

Chapter nineteen

Lydia's father had caught the early ferry as planned. He had the minimum number of documents with him. Because of his secret work he held several passports, and carried one with a false name, which had been provided to protect him. It was the same with his phone – the one he carried only had the numbers he needed in it; there was nothing that might reveal who he really was. Being Maltese by heritage, his colouring was dark and he blended well into the background, and was wearing clothes similar to those worn by the migrants. A minute camera and a microphone were attached to his clothes in inconspicuous places. He just needed to get firm evidence of people-smuggling crimes, enough to convict the people or persons concerned. He hoped this would be his last assignment and at the end of it the ringleaders would be behind bars.

John landed without problems and was through immigration and security checks easily, and soon on his way to the small town where he hoped to get his first contact. That part was easy, for most of the contact people were 'small fry' – not important in the organisation and generally not suspicious of the people who contacted them to buy a passage to Europe.

They met in a café and drank hot, sweet coffee together while the contact arranged a meeting with the 'boss' for lunchtime. That was better than John had hoped for – all being well, he would be on the early afternoon ferry back to Samos.

John walked to the main square in the town and sat under the tamarisk tree as instructed. He looked at the people milling around and wondered how many of them had walked for weeks or months to arrive at this place and had horrendous stories of war and persecution. How sad the world had become! If he could do just a little to make it a better place, he would be satisfied. That was why he had become involved with this work, and had even put his own family at risk. The thought of what had happened to Lydia made him angry – and he knew, if he was honest, there was an element of revenge in this mission. He knew he needed to keep that in check; he could make a fatal mistake if he allowed his personal feelings to influence his decisions.

The man called Cobra arrived. From Nakato's description, he was in no doubt this was the same man who had come to meet him.

'Follow me,' he was instructed, so he did just that, and the man led him through tiny alleyways and backstreets. John knew he would not easily find his way back, but one of the devices hidden on his person was for tracking. Eventually they reached a huge metal door. A guard let them in and John was taken to an office. He was questioned about where he had travelled from, and why; where he hoped to go; what personal papers he owned; and did he have American dollars? Years of working undercover had taught John to be very careful how he answered. He had practised trying to think as a migrant would and had expected these questions. So far, so good.

Cobra, though, was suspicious. He had dealt with hundreds of migrants, and somehow, something didn't quite fit about this man. For a start, he was on his own – no family leaving with him, and that was unusual. He looked too well-fed to be a migrant who had travelled a long way. Also, there was something about him which was familiar, but he couldn't place it.

'OK,' he said, speaking in English, 'you seem in a hurry to get to Europe. If you have the money with you, then I will keep you here until dark and you can cross to Samos tonight.'

Both men were eyeing each other up – the tension between them was palpable.

'I do have money, but your price is very high,' replied John, bargaining in the true Middle Eastern manner. They bargained together for a while, then agreed a price and John handed it over, plus his phone and false passport.

'Where do I meet the boat?' John asked. 'I would like to walk in the town and buy some food and water.'

'No need for that,' replied the man. 'I will supply both, and a life jacket. Come with me to a waiting room.'

John was slightly worried by this, but tried to show no emotion or he might raise suspicion. He allowed himself to be locked in a small room, and true to his word, the man had food, water and even a life jacket brought to him, but John knew he was, in fact, a prisoner. He tried to remain calm, acting as if he were pleased to be travelling to Europe that night. Thank goodness he hadn't been body-searched – and he prayed silently that it would not happen, though he did have concealed weapons if things became really nasty.

It was a long wait through the afternoon until darkness fell. Then John was put into the back of a car and driven away. He knew then that his cover had most likely been blown, for he had expected to be put into the back of a lorry, along with other migrants.

'Wondering why you are in my car, Captain Rocco?' Cobra asked him. 'I was suspicious when I first talked to you – then I had those dollars checked, and found they were all marked notes. Very clever of you, but you are not as clever as me! I do admit that I messed up a bit when I hit your daughter – I had hoped to kill her outright as revenge for your work, trying to sabotage our operation. Never mind, I'll take you out instead.'

John was seething, but he still tried to keep calm. He had managed to escape from difficult situations before. A henchman sitting next to him had a gun pointed at him, but as Cobra was still talking, he obviously hadn't yet been given the order to shoot. John slowly slid his hand into his pocket for one of his secret weapons. He took the protective sheath from a syringe and, leaning towards the henchman, he sneezed loudly and managed to push the needle through the man's shirt without being noticed and withdraw it quickly. He sneezed again.

'Oh dear, catching a cold, are we?' said Cobra. 'We can't have that, can we? I'll have to cover you up and keep you warm. Maybe a body bag would do!' He laughed loudly at his own joke. John kept his cool, as he had been trained to do. The man beside him was getting sleepy – the drug was working! He loosened his grip on the gun, and John removed it and slid it into his pocket. It was good that the boss was driving and so was not able to see all that was happening in the back.

At last they arrived at the cove, where a truck was waiting with many migrants.

The car stopped and Cobra said something in Turkish to the henchman, who was far too sleepy to answer or obey. Cobra angrily went to the back passenger door and opened it, only to have the man fall out. Cobra's hand went at once to his pocket to get his gun, but John was faster and shot his captor in the foot.

Cobra was taken by surprise and yelled out curses as he held his ankle. As he did so, John grabbed his gun. Suddenly they were surrounded by refugees who had jumped off the lorry. Everyone was excited and confused. The truck driver ran over and recognised his boss, who shouted out orders in Turkish. He spoke to the people, telling them to calm down and get in line, put on life jackets and be ready to board the boats. Then the injured Cobra began shouting orders to capture and kill the man who was in the car, but the only person they could see was the drugged henchman. Captain John Rocco was nowhere to be seen.

Chapter twenty

In the middle of the confusion, John managed to slip through the crowd and hide behind a rock. It had taken all the restraint he knew not to shoot to kill the man who had tried to murder his daughter. He had to think, and do it quickly. He needed to take the boss prisoner and get him to Samos, so that he could be brought to justice. He had no phone and was not sure how many of the crowd were migrants and who might be in the employ of the people smugglers. The lorry driver was marshalling people to line up for the boats. John slipped on his life jacket and joined the queue, with another syringe ready. He crept close enough to the driver to inject him, and with so many people milling around, he slipped away again easily.

Cobra was sitting on the ground, still barking out orders to his men, but the blood loss and pain were making him weaker. It was obvious that he was hurrying the boatmen and instructing them to get the boats away.

Meanwhile, Dave and Mike had been making their way down the cliff that rose above the cove and arrived in the middle of the mayhem. Somehow they sensed that John was involved in what was going on, so their primary aim was to locate him, but they were both recognisable as foreigners and knew they had to be careful. Their Scout training from years earlier came into their minds and helped them to see, but not be seen. As they surveyed the scene, Dave saw the injured man and crept up slowly behind him. He saw his tattooed arm and knew this was the notorious Cobra. Dave took a thick rope from around his waist, made a lasso and threw it over the boss' head and shoulders, securing his arms. Cobra thrashed around and swore, trying to turn around to see his attacker. Meanwhile, Mike had seen John in the crowd and ran to him.

'Don't board their boat,' he said quietly. 'Over the cliff and down in the next cove we have our dinghy waiting for you. We need to get out of Turkish waters before the patrol boat finds us.'

'You don't know how glad I am to see you, son,' said John. 'But I have to take care of Cobra, the person in charge of this whole operation, and somehow get him to a place where he'll be arrested and tried for his crimes.'

'I think Dave's well on the way to doing that,' chuckled Mike. 'Look over there.'

John looked and saw the boss, bound by a thick rope, and Dave kneeling by him bandaging his foot and stopping the blood loss. John had an idea. He went over, and plunged another syringe into Cobra. Soon the man was very weak and not struggling at all.

'Can we take him with us?' asked John. 'I'd like to shoot him with his own gun, which was meant for me, but I need to do this thing properly. He must be apprehended and then the appropriate authorities can deal with him.'

'We'll have to carry him to the dinghy – but we can try. With three against one we should manage it somehow,' replied Mike.

'We're medics!' Dave said to anyone who looked their way. 'This man is sick and injured. We can help him. But he's very ill and what he has could be contagious!'

People seemed to understand. Dave's warnings seemed to stop anyone coming too close, and between them they did manage to half-carry, half-drag Cobra to the dinghy.

'He'll be a spitting cobra now,' commented Mike, with irony, and as quickly as they could they pulled anchor and set off for Samos. The wind was favourable, and they slipped away without being noticed by the Turkish authorities. That wasn't surprising since they had seen the dinghies with the migrants setting off and the boats were very quickly getting into difficulties as they were so overloaded, so the authorities were busy trying to help them.

Cold, tired, wet and exhausted, the three men and their captive arrived on the beach near the hotel. They put down the anchor and secured the dinghy, then faced the final task of getting the injured man up the beach.

The twins ran to the hotel to get help and phone for the police and ambulance. Jane was sitting with the girls. They had been praying together. Hannah knew that her mother would have immediately turned to God for help in any crisis, and she suggested they all asked God to help. They were terrified that John might never come back – they knew he had been on a dangerous mission and that it had something to do with Nakato.

When the police arrived about the same time as the ambulance, the hotel proprietor translated for John as he explained who he was and all about the prisoner. John asked for a phone and contacted his head office, telling them how the mission had gone. They asked for an armed guard to be provided to watch over the prisoner until officials from the UK were flown out to deal with the situation. John explained that Cobra faced, among others, charges of attempted murder, and extradition orders would be sought. The Greek police were very helpful, and a still-dazed Cobra was taken under armed escort to the hospital.

Finally, John was free to sit down with the two boys, Hannah and his family, and explain as much of his secret mission as he knew was permissible. They all needed to know the truth and that the threat to their lives was now over. The newspaper for which he worked had already accepted his resignation – this had been his last mission.

'At last, one of the main ringleaders of the people-smuggling outfit in Turkey has been apprehended, and the secret services will certainly make him reveal all he knows about others in the same trade. In my experience, these thugs, once they are caught, are cowards, and keen to protect their own skins,' John told them. 'Now we had all better get some sleep. I can't thank you boys enough for all your help. Had I come back in an overloaded boat I might have been lost at sea or been caught by the Turkish authorities. I think Cobra's plan had been to shoot me and dump me overboard.'

Chapter twenty-one

Early the next morning, the RAF flew in some secret service officials. They had a meeting with John and then interviewed the twins. After this, Dave took one of the men to talk to Nakato and the Pakistani family, to hear their stories. Meanwhile, the girls were relaxing and enjoying the beach and the regatta, Hannah sailing with Mike and making second place, while Lydia and Jane cheered them on. They wanted to make the most of the short time left to them before they returned to England.

'It's strange,' said Lydia. 'I feel somehow much lighter inside. I think the worry of the death threat was playing on my mind.'

'Not only yours, Lyd,' responded Hannah, 'mine and your parents' too. I think all of us were worried that man would try to harm you again, especially after that letter came through your door.'

'Hey, Lydia,' called out Dave, as he came through the terrace and down to the pool to find her. 'I've just learned some great news. Wait until you hear this. You'll want to dance, even with casts on your legs!'

'What is it?' laughed Lydia – Dave's jokes always made her laugh.

'I've just been speaking to one of the guys from London. He wanted to see Nakato, then he made some phone calls and she is to be transferred to a hospital in London, as soon as a flight can be arranged, to have the operation she needs. Meanwhile, an application for a visa will be filed. She's been accepted under a special charity medical scheme, so her medical bills will be paid for her.'

Lydia's eyes filled with tears – she was crying with joy that her friend would get help. If only her brother, Musome, could hear the news; how happy he and his university friends would be.

'Please can I visit her there, so she doesn't feel so alone?' she asked her mum, who had joined the girls. 'She'll need so much support.'

Jane's instant response was, 'Of course, sweetheart, and if she needs it, our home will be open to her.'

'She may indeed need that,' said Dave. 'The official told her she might be asked to be a witness if Cobra is brought to the UK for trial, and a visa granted for her to remain in the UK on a long-term basis. It is a great help that she had a relative who served in the King's African Rifles in the Second World War.'

Later in the day, Cobra was duly escorted, after treatment for his wound, from Samos hospital and put into prison on the Greek mainland while the extradition process began. Somehow, it was good to know that he was no longer on the island.

That evening's entertainment, after the presentation of sailing certificates, was to take any guests who wished to go, to a cinema. It wasn't a regular theatre at all, but in a village, high in the hills, where a family had turned their back garden into an open-air cinema. The film was projected on to a white wall at the bottom of the garden and there were white plastic chairs for guests to sit on while the family sold snacks and drinks before the film started. The atmosphere was very relaxed and noisy as families and friends gathered and socialised together.

It was Friday evening, and on Fridays the film presented was always in English. The films were not blockbusters, and Hannah and Lydia had not heard of the film showing that night, *The Man Who Knew Infinity*, but the whole atmosphere was friendly, and they found the true story of a poorly educated Indian man who could do incredible mathematical equations very interesting.

During the interval, the grandmother and mother of the family who ran the cinema came around and offered the audience sticky little doughnuts covered in honey, which they had made. They were included in the entrance fee and part of the whole experience.

'I can't resist these Greek treats with honey,' remarked Hannah, as she took her second doughnut.

'We can see that,' laughed Mike. 'The honey is all round your mouth. I think I'd better kiss it away!'

'Cheeky,' responded Hannah, but held her lips towards him and was rewarded by a sticky kiss.

'Hey, you two are as bad as each other – both covered in honey. Want a tissue?' asked Dave. 'Or maybe you just want another free doughnut each.'

'It's amazing that they've made so many and they are all free,' said Lydia. 'It's a real midnight feast. We'd better settle down again, the lights are dimming.'

'I'm glad about that,' answered Hannah. 'The mosquitoes have been eating my legs like crazy while the lights were on. Have any of you got any "after sting" cream?'

'Wish I had,' replied Mike. 'I'd gladly rub it on your legs!'

'Maybe I'm glad I still have plaster casts on mine,' quipped Lydia, as they got comfortable for the supporting short film, which was a cartoon. It was just what they needed to end a fun evening.

Afterwards, it took a few minutes for everyone to get back on the hotel's minibus, and it was almost 1am by the time they all arrived back at the hotel. Mike walked Hannah back to the room, while Dave pushed Lydia. They made a good foursome. Lydia wished it could last – but they had to return home the following evening.

'Hannah, can we have one last sail together tomorrow morning?' Mike asked her.

'I'd love that,' she whispered back and he gave her a little kiss on the cheek, keeping hold of her hand a little longer than he needed to. How tingly he made her feel! If only their friendship could last – but she feared that once she was back at college, Mike would move on to his winter sports venue and forget all about her.

Dave had stopped pushing Lydia, to give his brother and Hannah a little space to say goodnight. They waited under a tamarisk tree, Dave sitting on a little wall so that he was the same level as Lydia.

'Lydia,' he said, 'you are so beautiful. Your scars only make your inner beauty shine out more. Please can we stay friends? When I'm in London studying – and I fly over next week – would you mind if I visited you and we could go out sometimes? I promise I will take great care of you.'

Lydia was taken by surprise. It was a good job it was dark, because she was blushing furiously. She hardly dared look up at Dave, into his gentle and kind face, but answered, 'I would so love that – but I am a burden. I'm still not supposed be left on my own, in case of a sudden fit. Are you sure you want to be with me?'

'Lydia, you are not a burden, and you never will be. I've promised that I will take care of you. I know you have to be escorted everywhere, but that will be a pleasure. I love hanging out with you. There's something else, too. You remember you told me about your near-death experience and the voice that said it wasn't time for you to leave earth yet? I know that you want to learn more about God, and so do I. Even Nakato's story has helped me to understand more about the love and care of God for each of us. She talked about God and Jesus a lot when she told her story to the RAF guys. Could we begin a faith journey together?' Dave asked quietly, but with great sincerity.

'I know so little, but I'm sure Hannah's mum, Auntie Pauline, will help me learn. She goes to a church and the people there prayed for me when I was hanging between life and death. Hannah and I have both decided that once we're back home, starting next Sunday, we're going to go there. Nakato's story touched me deeply, too. I want to visit her when she's in hospital and then I hope she can live with us afterwards. She will need a home and a family to care for her – she's only a year older than me. Maybe she can get some more education. Although she only went to primary school, she is very clever. The man in the film this evening made me think of her – how far she could go if she had the opportunity.'

Dave saw Mike leaving the doorway of the room, so he gave Lydia a kiss on her forehead and once again whispered to her that he thought she was beautiful. Tears filled her eyes, and she managed to whisper, 'Thank you,' and, 'See you tomorrow,' as he helped her out of the chair and on to her crutches and into the room.

The girls didn't sleep much that night, but lay on their beds talking about the twins, admitting that they were both smitten by them.

'I wonder if I'll see Mike again,' said Hannah, with a sigh. 'At least Dave has asked if he can take you out and he'll be in London soon. Mike will be miles away in the French Alps. I'm going to miss him so much.'

'If he really cares about you, then he'll keep in contact, and that's easy by phone and WhatsApp. He's not as shallow as Sam was,' Lydia answered, trying to comfort her friend.

Then they chatted about Nakato, and Lydia told Hannah that she wanted her parents to let her live with them after the operation.

'You wouldn't mind, would you?' she asked Hannah. 'You'll always be my best friend, but I know she needs friends and support. She's been through so much.'

'I think it would be lovely. Maybe she would come with us to church – you told me she's been asking questions about God and Jesus. We could all learn together.'

'Dave wants to learn about God and things like that, too,' Lydia told her friend. 'He suggested we could start a spiritual journey together.'

The next morning Hannah went sailing with Mike.

'I'm glad we can have this last sail together, Hannah,' Mike said to her. 'I know that I'm always joking, and that's the way I am, but I want to talk to you seriously.'

Hannah's heart sank. Was he going to tell her that he'd had fun and enjoyed being with her, but now it was over? She looked up at him, and his eyes were no longer laughing as they usually were.

'What is it?' she asked. 'What's on your mind?'

'Well, Hannah, the answer to that is easy – it's you. Well, you and me. I don't quite know how to say this, but... umm... I want to stay in touch with you. I know I've got a reputation for being a flirt and you might not trust me, but I really feel something for you. I know I'm older than you and you have lots of studying to do, but would you stay in touch?'

Hannah was so taken by surprise and had been so sure that he wanted to finish their friendship that she took a few moments to answer.

'Oh, Mike,' she said, beaming all over her face. 'I would *love* our friendship to go on. I was afraid you wanted it to finish. I have been dreading the thought that when we leave tonight I might never see you again, that you would go to France and find a beautiful girlfriend and forget all about me.'

Mike leaned forward and gave her a kiss which certainly reassured her that he did care, even if it made the dinghy almost capsize!

Dave came to sit by the pool with Lydia. He had said what had been on his heart the evening before, and was just happy to be in her company. She was sketching the tamarind trees – just a pencil drawing, but it was good.

'Hey, Lydia,' he said. 'That's such a great drawing. Would you let me have it? I'd like to frame it and put it on my wall, to remind me of Samos and of you.'

'It's not that good, Dave,' she responded, 'but of course you can have it. I'll do you a painting when we get home, hopefully one that will be worth keeping.'

'Thanks, but I'll still always treasure this. You're really good at art. Maybe you should think of studying that as a career.'

'I will be doing A level Art, but I'm not sure I'm good enough to make it a career. I'm not like Hannah, who's brilliant at music and has always wanted to do that at uni,' she answered. 'I did wonder about nursing. Mum is a terrific nurse, and I think I'd like it, but I may not be fit enough for that. Perhaps I'll think more about doing an art degree.'

Lydia's parents had gone for a stroll along the beach. They had not really spent much time together through the holiday. It had turned out to be rather different than they had planned. Jane had to return to work, as well as Hannah to college. John knew, as well, that once he had put Jane, Lydia and Hannah on the plane, he must rejoin his ship and get back to work. A helicopter would be waiting at the airport to take him back to sea. At least he knew the threat to his family had been dealt with and he was much happier about them returning to Croydon.

'What an eventful holiday it's been!' he said to his wife. 'You need to go home for a rest, not back to work. You can stop worrying now. My assignment with the paper is finished and I'll never put you in such danger again.

'I did wonder, though, what you felt about Nakato? When she's discharged from hospital, are you happy about her staying with us?'

'I was going to ask you the same question!' replied Jane.

'It could be for a long time.'

'Yes. I know Lydia would love to have her around and it will be another person in the house when I'm at work. I do worry about Lydia needing company, in case she has a fit. I can't expect my parents to always look after her. It's not fair on them as they're getting older.'

'We'll sound out Lydia at lunchtime. I'm so glad you're happy about it, dear. It looks as if Lydia may have also found an admirer. Dave is quite taken with her. I can see it in his eyes!'

'She's only sixteen,' replied Jane. 'That's very young. She has a lot of schooling to finish and Dave has seven years of medical studies ahead of him.'

'You were only sweet sixteen when I met you, and we waited!' John reminded her.

'Maybe you're right – we'll have to wait and see,' Jane replied, giving her husband the lovely smile which had won his heart so many years before. 'Somehow I feel that this holiday has been like the closing of a chapter of our lives. We have all been changed by the experiences of the last few months, and Lydia has been so brave and grown up so much. Now she's ready to go to college, choose a career, have boyfriends and make her own decisions. It will be great to see what life has in store for her. I'm so glad she has good friends like Hannah and Dave. It's time for us to let her go.'

Chapter twenty-two

The girls felt sad that evening as they finished packing their cases, ready to go to the airport. Of course, they knew that the holiday would have to come to an end, but in spite of Lydia's fit, it had been such a special time, especially getting to know Mike and Dave.

'All good things have to come to an end,' said John, as he helped his wife and the girls into the car. As it was the end of the summer season, and almost all the guests had gone home, the boys were also free to take a taxi and see the girls safely on their way. Even though the death threat to Lydia's life was no longer an issue, the chartered RAF plane was still going to take them home. It had been organised by the secret services in conjunction with the newspaper.

As they were waiting, chatting together in the airport foyer, another car drove up. Escorted by Pam, the Englishwoman who helped the refugees, Nakato got out. Lydia was so delighted to see her friend, she rushed over and gave her a huge hug.

'Are you coming to England with us?' she asked.

'Yes, she is,' answered Pam. 'When we tried to arrange an emergency medical flight through the RAF, we found this flight was taking you and had room for Nakato, too. That was wonderful because it meant that you could be the escorts. When you arrive at the RAF station in Wiltshire tonight, you will be given accommodation, then early Sunday morning an ambulance car will collect Nakato to take her to the Elizabeth Garrett Anderson Wing of University College Hospital in London.'

Pam gave the travelling documents to Jane and asked her to look after Nakato.

Once their luggage had been checked and loaded, Jane and the girls said their final goodbyes and boarded the plane. Lydia had help up the steps. How she wished it was Dave's strong arm supporting her instead of the RAF airman's. Her dad and the twins were on a balcony and waved and blew kisses to them all.

Nakato was scared as she went into the plane.

'I've never been in a plane and I'm frightened,' she said to Lydia, quietly. 'I feel scared about going to Europe, even though that has been my dream for many months.'

'When we came out here it was the first time that Hannah had been in a plane, too,' Lydia told her, 'and she loved it. Would you like to sit by the window, and I'll be next to you, Hannah the other side of the aisle and Mum next to her?'

Once Nakato had settled in the seat, Lydia showed her how to fasten the seat belt.

'There will be a lot of noise from the engines as we take off, but don't be worried, that's normal,' she explained.

'Once we're above the clouds and at the right height, it's much quieter.'

'Will you hold my hand?' Nakato asked when they were told to be ready for the take-off.

Lydia reached over to her friend, gave her a sweet to suck, then gently took her hand. Once they were up in the sky, Nakato relaxed and looked in amazement at the beauty of the clouds and the setting sun. Soon, it became dark and, after all the excitement of the day, the girls and Jane all dozed off and they slept for most of the journey.

As they landed, Lydia looked after Nakato and explained what was happening, especially when the undercarriage opened to release the wheels and made quite a noise.

As they touched down, they were surprised by lights and cameras flashing, and a reception committee.

'What's going on?' Jane asked the airman who had been looking after them.

'I don't know,' he answered. 'I'll see if I can find out.'

Once the steps had been pushed up to the plane, he went to find out what all the fuss was about and was told that the press had heard about Nakato and wanted photos.

Poor Nakato was scared. 'Why do they want my photo?' she asked. 'What is wrong?' She wished she still had her burka to wear – it would have covered her face.

Jane tried to protect the girls and refused to let any of them be interviewed, but did confirm that Nakato had been rescued trying to cross the sea as a migrant, and was being flown to the UK for urgent medical treatment.

Lydia in her wheelchair, Hannah and Jane were included in the photo as 'friends who had helped her in Samos and accompanied her to the UK'.

They were quickly taken into the airbase and given a meal, then made comfortable for the night. The three girls shared a room, with Jane in one next to theirs. The girls chatted for a little while, then dropped off to sleep. It was a good thing that Jane had set the alarm on her phone, for the girls were still asleep when they were called for breakfast.

'Now you'll have to get used to our culture and food,' stated Lydia cheerfully, as they surveyed the array of food available at the officers' mess, where they were taken for breakfast. 'Let me explain about these foods and you can choose what you think you will like.'

They walked over to the buffet of cooked food and Lydia explained that bacon and sausages were both from pigs, knowing that, having been brought up as a Moslem, Nakato would not have tasted pork or other meats from the pig. In the end, they both decided to have scrambled eggs on toast.

On the table there was toast, butter, marmalade and jam – and Nakato wanted to taste them all.

'I have a lot to learn in this new country,' she said. 'I hope I will be allowed to stay here.'

'We hope so, too,' said Jane, 'and we want you to know, Nakato, that for however long you are in this country, our home will always be your home. After the operation, we would like you to come and be Lydia's Ugandan sister.'

Nakato was beside herself with happiness – she knew no one in England and had had no idea what she would do once she arrived! Now she had a home and a family. Now she knew that Jesus must love her, for He had answered her prayers. If only her brother and his friends could know she was safe!

Far away in Kampala, a group of students at Makere University were about to go to the church service. They were in the Students' Union drinking coffee and watching football on the television. Suddenly there came a newsflash – an item about a Ugandan girl. Musome watched and saw his sister coming out of an RAF plane in England. Tears ran down his face – everyone was looking at him, but he didn't mind.

'She made it; she made it!' he shouted. 'Thank God she is safe!'

'Shut up and listen!' someone said to him, and he quietened and heard how Nakato had been rescued from the sea, escaping from Turkey, and had been flown to England for an operation. For security reasons, her true name wasn't given, for she was to be a witness in the trial of a people smuggler who, because of her help, had been captured.

The students went to church and spread the wonderful news that all their fundraising and their subsequent prayers had not been in vain. Musome's sister was safe and sound in England, and would receive the operation she needed! It was the most wonderful news, and the church members spent the next hour thanking and praising God.

'Obviously, God had a different plan from the one we devised to get her to Ethiopia and then to Europe!' said Musome. 'I hope she writes soon so that we can learn the whole story and give glory to God. Alleluia!' and he started jumping in the air and doing traditional Ugandan dancing. 'God must have had it put on the television so that we could see it and know she was safe – isn't that just amazing?'

That Sunday morning, tired though they were, Hannah and Lydia kept their promise to God and went to church along with Hannah's parents. They sat at the back and tried not to be noticed, but when a whole group of young people came in and saw them, they insisted that the girls sit with them. Afterwards they were told all about the youth activities and really made to feel welcome.

The following Friday evening there was to be a barbecue, the last one of the season, they were told, followed by a DVD. Would they like to come? The youth leader promised to collect Lydia as she would need her wheelchair. Lydia agreed, for she was sure that her mother wouldn't mind, especially as there was transport both ways. Hannah promised to come to Lydia's house and travel with her. It seemed that now they had made a move towards God, He was running with open arms to them, and they were excited about it all.

After church and a quick lunch, Jane drove the girls up to the hospital in London. It was so much easier to drive there on a Sunday, as the roads were quieter, and they wanted to make sure that Nakato had settled in and wasn't feeling too isolated. They had a bag of toiletries, towels and night clothes for Nakato. Jane had a spare mobile phone which she had charged up and into which she had put Lydia's and Hannah's numbers, as well as her own. It was for Nakato; that way they could keep in close touch and know if she needed anything.

Nakato was so thrilled to see them – and completely overwhelmed by their gifts. They pulled the curtains around the bed and she changed into a pretty pair of pyjamas. It was good to be out of the hospital gown which she had been given.

'Look at me,' she said in delight. 'Now I look like other people in the ward. I feel so smart. These clothes for bed are so, how do you say it? Cool?'

'Yes, you really do look cool,' Lydia agreed. 'Mum has brought something else for you, a mobile phone, so you can talk to us all and tell us if you need anything.'

'A phone? For me?' questioned Nakato, amazed to think that she would own a mobile. Jane and the girls spent most of the rest of the visiting time showing her how to use the phone. It took quite a while as it was a completely new thing to learn about. It was a simple phone without many features, but it did have a camera and this really fascinated Nakato. She wanted to take photos of Lydia, Hannah and Jane at once, so that she could look at them every day.

Lydia laughed with her as Nakato told her that this hospital wasn't so strict about 'rules' – and the LUL was managed because the nurses had given her special underwear and pads, but the next day she would have the operation.

'I am so happy because I am not alone. You and Hannah and your parents are my friends. Do you know, I even found a book about God and Jesus in the cupboard by the bed? He must love me to put a book there!'

'Let me see,' said Lydia, and Nakato showed her a Bible.

'Oh, that's cool,' remarked Hannah, leaning over to see. 'Start reading at St Mark – look, I'll find it for you. That will tell you about Jesus.' Hannah put a piece of paper in the place for Nakato.

'The nurses here call me Katy. They say that's an English name like mine and easier to remember,' she told her visitors.

'When you leave the hospital and come to live with us, would you like to be called Katy?' Jane asked her. 'It might be easier for Lydia's grandparents to call you that.'

'Will I have a *jaaja*, too?' asked Nakato, then she remembered she had used a Ugandan word for grandparent – and added, 'I mean a grandmother.'

'You bet,' replied Lydia, 'I call them Gran and Gramps, but I'm sure they won't mind being called Ja or whatever you said.'

'*Jaaja* – yes, I'd love to call them that: *Jaaja* Gran and *Jaaja* Gramps, will that do?'

'I think that will be great!' said Lydia, with a smile.

Chapter twenty-three

The next week Hannah started at college. It seemed as if she had been away for months, not days. She tried hard to forget all the excitement and concentrate on her work. She had a lot of music practice to catch up on, too, as a flute exam was coming up. She found her mind kept wandering and thinking about Mike. Was he missing her? Maybe he had already found another girl. In her heart of hearts, she hoped he hadn't. Joe, her partner at the school leavers' prom, asked her for a date on her first day back, but she declined. In her mind, Mike was her boyfriend, and even though Joe was a nice boy, she didn't feel any thrill when he was around her.

It was strange for Lydia when the casts were taken off her legs a few days after they arrived home. Her muscles had become so weak that she needed to have physiotherapy to strengthen them. She was determined to get fit again as soon as possible, so she practised the exercises several times each day. Her mum was continuing to work part-time until Lydia was steady on her feet again, so as often as possible they went to visit Nakato. The train journey was quite straightforward from East Croydon, and they enjoyed the trips together. They went in the morning, did a little shopping, had lunch and then went to see Katy, as they were trying to remember to call her. Her operation had been a success, but she had to stay there for a while afterwards, since she had had major reconstruction and needed post-operative care. It helped that Jane was a nurse, because she would be able to continue Katy's care after discharge.

All Katy's papers to stay in the country had to be put into order, too. Since she was to be a witness at the trial of Cobra, who had been transferred to a prison somewhere in the UK, Nakato was under the care of a government agency who dealt with such things, making sure she was protected.

During her visits to Katy, Lydia was fascinated to find out why the hospital had such a long name. She found out that it had a long history, too. One afternoon the ward was very quiet and the nurses were spending time chatting to their patients.

'Who was Elizabeth Garrett Anderson?' Lydia asked one of the nurses.

'A very inspiring lady,' the nurse told them. 'She lived in the late nineteenth century, and died in 1917. She was the very first woman in Britain to become a physician and a surgeon, and she founded the New Hospital for Women, establishing a training school for women to become doctors. She herself had not been allowed into the medical schools and had been trained privately by some medics who she persuaded to help her. Later, the hospital was renamed "Elizabeth Garrett Anderson Hospital" in her honour, but was eventually demolished and incorporated into UCH.'

'She sounds like an amazing woman,' remarked Katy.

'She really was,' the nurse told them. 'She not only pioneered medicine as a career for women, but she also took up the cause of women as a suffragette, helping women to get the vote. She was a strong, gutsy woman, just like you, Katy. You could have given up on your journey many times, but you were strong, and here you are in England. I'm sure you'll have a great future. Maybe you'll be able to fight against FGM and make a difference in your home country.'

'Wow,' Nakato replied. 'What a thought. It would be so wonderful to stop other girls being cut and suffering as I did. Maybe that's why God brought me here safely.'

One day, just a day or so before Katy was due to be discharged, Lydia's phone rang. When she looked at the number, her heart jumped for joy and she instantly recognised the voice.

'Dave!' she said. 'How great to hear you. Where are you? In Samos?'

'I'm on the train to East Croydon,' he answered. 'How do I get to your house?'

Lydia was so excited. Although the days since they had returned from Samos had been very busy, she hadn't forgotten him and was longing to hear from him again. Hannah had been getting texts and calls from Mike and she had been feeling a bit disappointed that she hadn't heard from Dave.

She told him which bus to catch from outside the station and where to get off. 'I'll come to the bus stop and meet you,' she added.

Dave was now in London and apologised for not being in contact sooner, but explained about going to see his parents, then having to report to his university in London, and settle into the hall of residence; this was the first free day he had had.

'Hey, I hope you don't mind me surprising you like this,' he said, giving Lydia a beautiful bunch of roses. 'I couldn't wait any longer, so on the spur of the moment I jumped on a train, and just prayed you would be at home and free.'

'Of course I don't mind,' Lydia replied, blushing a bit as she took the roses and thanked him. 'Mum is at work, but Gran is at home. I've not had any more fits, but as the medicine is still being reduced gradually, someone is still around with me. Very soon Nakato will be home, so then I'll have company all the time.'

'It's great to see your legs,' commented Dave, in a teasing voice, 'and I just love your hairstyle.'

Lydia's short hair had been styled nicely. 'I miss my long hair, but it will grow again. I hope to grow a fringe, too, to cover some of the scars – but I feel more "normal" now that I can walk around without casts.'

Gran had the kettle on and was busy making lunch. She didn't miss the way this young man looked at her granddaughter with admiration.

Although it had only been a couple of weeks since Lydia had left Samos, there was so much to talk about and catch up on. After they had eaten some lunch, she sent a text to

Hannah, to tell her that Dave was at her house, and suggested she called in on her way home from college.

'I've got a letter with me from Mike,' Dave told her. 'I'm so glad that he's written to her. He's really smitten! He says he hasn't flirted with any other girl since Hannah left, and I believe him. He's even told Dad and Mum that he's found a gorgeous girlfriend – so he must be serious.'

Hannah arrived as soon as she could escape from her classes, and her first question was about Mike.

'How's Mike? When will he be back here?' she asked, as she took the letter Dave handed her. Inside, along with a card, was a pressed flower. She was thrilled – emails and texts were great to receive, but a handwritten card with a flower was something else! Hannah put it in her bag to read it privately, and thought she would keep the pressed rose in her Bible.

'Mike will be home at the end of this week,' Dave informed Hannah. 'He'll go to see our parents, then is coming to London to stay with me for a while, before he heads back to work at the winter resort. Don't worry, he'll be in touch as soon as he's here.'

'We'll be able to go out as a foursome again,' Hannah said, in delight.

'But we will be five,' said Lydia. 'Nakato will be living with us by then, we can't leave her out!'

'Hey, don't worry, Lydia, we won't,' said Dave. 'It'll be great. We'll all have fun together. Until I start ward work, my weekends will be free. I'd love to spend as much time with you as I can.'

After Hannah had gone home, Dave asked Lydia if he could take her out that evening for dinner.

'Let me text Mum and tell her,' she said. 'She's working until seven today. Where would you like to go?'

'You choose,' Dave answered at once. 'Wherever you like. I don't know anywhere in Croydon. Somewhere quiet and cosy, so that we can really talk. I've missed you so much, Lydia. That's why I took the chance and jumped on a train this morning. I like Hannah and it was great to see her, but this time I just want us to have some time together on our own. Is that OK?'

'Of course,' she replied, with the shy smile he loved so much. 'I'll get Gran to make you a cup of tea while I get changed. There's a lovely restaurant in the woods at Shirley, not far from here. Dad and Mum go there when they want a quiet meal alone. The phone number will be here somewhere.'

They had a lovely evening together. There was so much to talk about. Dave wanted to know all about Nakato and how the surgery went, and about her recovery.

'She wants to be called Katy, now,' explained Lydia. 'The nurses started to call her that and she likes it, because it's more English. As soon as she comes out of hospital, she's coming to live with us for as long as she needs a home.'

'How do you really feel about that?' Dave asked. 'Do you mind sharing your family and home on a long-term basis?'

'At first, I thought the idea was wonderful,' answered Lydia, thoughtfully. 'Then I did worry about how I would feel, having a sister all the time. I've been an only child, and my parents and grandparents spoil me and have always given me lots of time. I realise that I'll have to adjust and share lots of things, though we will each have our own room. I could feel jealous – so I started to pray about it. You know about God sending me back to earth when I was so ill. I'm sure that one reason for me still being alive is to help Katy.'

Lydia paused for a few minutes, and then continued. 'One day, when I was visiting Katy, soon after her operation, one of the nurses talked to us. I wondered why the unit was called "The Elizabeth Garrett Anderson Wing" and asked her who the lady was. She told us the story of Elizabeth, who studied privately because no medical school would admit women, and how she became the first registered female physician and surgeon. Then she founded a hospital for women and began to train women doctors. She was such an amazing woman, and the nurse looked at Katy and told her that she was a strong woman, too, and maybe could one day return to Uganda and try to change the culture among the Pokot people so that FGM would become a historic practice. Then I asked God how I could help Katy to achieve something like this, since she has not had a lot of education.'

'Hey, that's really cool,' answered Dave. 'Did you get an answer?'

'Thoughts came into my mind. I was hoping to start college after Christmas, but then I thought that I could help Katy study at home and catch up, and perhaps we could both go to college next September. I know it will mean I'll be a year behind with my studies, but it would be worth it to help her.'

'Lydia, you are so unselfish,' said Dave, reaching out to hold her hand over the table. 'I really think the world of you, and I took you out this evening to ask you if you would consider being my girlfriend. I know there's a difference in our ages and I have so many years of study ahead. How do you feel? I'll understand if you feel it's too soon to consider anything so serious. I may not be able to take you out on as many dates as I would like, because of study, long hours on the wards and not much money, but I promise I'll be there for you and give you as a good a time as I can.'

Lydia looked up into Dave's eyes. They were so gentle and sincere, she knew she could trust him. She was young, and it would be a long time to wait until Dave had qualified, but she knew that her feelings for him were already running deep in her heart. Then, too, she wanted to study and make something of her life.

As she looked at him and thought about his question, his heart was thumping so loudly that he was sure she could hear it.

'Yes, Dave, I would be so happy to be your girlfriend,' she replied. 'I can't deny the feelings I have for you. If you are sure that you really don't mind about my facial scars and the fact that I might have epilepsy for the rest of my life, then my answer is yes. I have a lot of studying ahead of me, too. If we are busy, then the time will pass quickly.'

'Lydia, I don't want to hear about your scars again. I don't even see them when I look at you. You are so beautiful inside and it shines on the outside. As for the epilepsy – if a doctor can't cope with that, then he shouldn't enter the profession. It's part of who you are and that's the person I care deeply about.' Dave squeezed her hand gently and leaned over to kiss her cheek. 'One other thing before I take you home,' he said. 'I am serious about following Jesus. I have bought a Bible and started to read the Gospels. At weekends, if I can get down here, I'd like to go to church with you and Hannah. Would that be possible?'

'That's more than possible – that's wonderful!' answered Lydia, her face alight with joy. 'What about Mike? I know Hannah has the hots for him, but now she's really following Jesus and has asked to be baptised. If Mike doesn't feel the same, it will be awful.'

'Mike is coming down next week – will you pray for me? I need to explain to him that I want to become a Christian and so do you and Hannah. Maybe it will open up a discussion between us. Whatever Hannah feels, tell her not to preach at Mike, but just to tell him that she wants to follow Jesus. He'll think about it, and we can pray for him,' replied Dave, seriously, as they put on their coats and left the restaurant.

Chapter twenty-four

Very soon after Dave's visit to Lydia, Katy was discharged from hospital and made her home with the Rocco family. Hannah had helped Lydia 'make over' the spare bedroom. They very enthusiastically set about painting it in 'girly' colours. Neither of them had decorated a room before, but they managed quite well.

'You look as mauve as the walls!' laughed Hannah, as she looked at Lydia's T-shirt and old jeans.

'You're not much better,' retorted Lydia. 'You have mauve hair and you've not even dyed it!'

'Actually, even my mouth tastes of paint,' admitted Hannah, 'but the walls do look nice.'

'We can go and buy some curtains and a duvet set to match, if you have time this afternoon,' Lydia told her. 'Won't Katy be surprised when she sees her room?! I've got some nice "smellies" for her and I've been choosing some books which I think she'll like.'

'It's not just Katy who will be surprised, but the twins are coming next weekend, and I think they'll be amazed at what we've done,' replied Hannah. 'I've been texting and phoning Mike about all the fun we're having.'

'Me, too – Dave, I mean,' laughed Lydia, 'and isn't Gran fantastic – she's letting the twins stay at her house any time they want to sleep over. I'm so lucky to have such wonderful grandparents who live so near.'

'It's fun being a foursome,' Hannah commented. 'I do wish Mike wasn't going back to work so soon. He won't even be home for Christmas.'

'He will see you baptised, though,' answered Lydia. 'He's promised you that.'

'Yes, and that is an answer to my prayers. I so want him to want to know Jesus, and hope my baptism will help him to understand how much Jesus means to me now,' Hannah replied, with a sigh.

'Dave and I are praying, too. Even my dad will be home that weekend, so we'll all be there for you. It will be a wonderful day.'

When Katy arrived in her new home, she was overwhelmed. To have a room of her own, and so pretty – she just couldn't find words to express how grateful she felt. Sometimes she just felt overcome with shyness; the home, food, kindness and whole culture was so completely different, she found it hard to take it all in. When Dave and Mike were visiting, they made sure that she was included in everything they did, and Katy also found that hard. Moslem culture was so different and she was scared when she was in the presence of men. She did enjoy going to church on Sundays, and the youth group were very happy to make friends. There were a few other young people from different ethnic backgrounds, including a girl from Kenya, with whom she could talk a bit in Swahili. Her Swahili wasn't that good – her English was better than her African second language – but it made her feel 'African' still.

Within a few days of Katy's coming to live in Croydon, she and Lydia decided to have school lessons together from Monday to Friday each week. One of the leaders of the youth group was a teacher, who taught year six in the local primary school. She offered to help Lydia by preparing some lessons for Katy. She was also qualified to teach English as a second language, and that was a great help.

The very first lesson they did together was to write a letter to Musome and describe, as fully as possible, Katy's adventures as she travelled to Britain. She wanted to tell her brother everything. It took a long time, but afterwards Katy told Lydia that she felt so much better now she had written it all. When writing about some of the horrible things that happened, she cried a lot, but it helped her to lay it to rest and gave her peace. At the end of the letter she told her brother that she, too, was now following Jesus. She knew he would be happy to hear that.

'Please write back to me at my new address,' she wrote at the end. 'Please tell me news from home, and thank your friends so much. One day, I am sure I will go back to Uganda, because I want to help stop FGM and also child marriage in our country.'

Lydia loved teaching Katy, and Katy loved to learn. They were very disciplined and worked normal school hours. Katy was quick to learn, and with the support from the teacher, she was soon catching up in almost every subject. They also found out that the sixth form college had some courses which might be suitable for Katy, as long as she could pass English and Maths at GCSE, so they focused very much on these two subjects.

In due course, the trial of Cobra began. This was a very scary time for both Katy and Lydia, but the family and church friends were supporting them. After some preliminary proceedings, the case was deferred for several months, but as the man was refused bail, the girls felt safe. Katy had been told that her papers would allow her to stay in Britain for the time being, and an application for immigration was being considered.

Christmas was approaching and Jane was looking forward to having her husband join them. He was rarely free to take leave at that time of year, as the cruise ship was always busy, but in view of all the trauma, the company agreed he should be at home. Katy was incredibly excited – everything was so new to her. Hannah and Lydia took her shopping, for she had the same amount of pocket money as Lydia and, so far, had saved it all. Lydia explained all the British customs and tried to teach her about celebrating the birth of Christ, and then all the other fun things which have grown up around these festivities, through the centuries. In researching this, Lydia learned a lot herself.

Just before Christmas, Dave had asked Lydia if she would accompany him to the university ball. She was very hesitant, still feeling self-conscious of her scars and worried in case the excitement might trigger a fit, but he promised he would come and collect her and take her to

London, then bring her home afterwards in a taxi, then stay the rest of the night with Gran and Gramps.

'What shall I wear?' she asked her mum. 'I think it will be very formal dress.'

'Why don't you wear Gran's dress again? You looked so beautiful in that – maybe it would please her to see you wear it to a Christmas ball, just as she did all those years ago.'

When her mum put it in that way, Lydia decided that she would wear the dress. When she told her grandparents, Gran's eyes filled with tears.

'I'm so glad, Dia,' she said. 'My special gown for my special granddaughter, to be worn at another Christmas ball.'

Hannah came and helped her friend get ready for the ball. She did her make-up with some special concealer which made the biggest scar look far less noticeable. Her hair was styled with a bit of a fringe which also hid the top of the scar. She looked amazing.

'You know, Lyd,' her friend told her, 'you look even more beautiful than last July. You have matured so much, you have much more poise. You'll knock the socks off Dave! Have a wonderful time and come back and tell us all about it – every little bit.'

'Me, too,' said Katy. 'I want to hear all about it. You are the best sister I could have, and so pretty.'

When Dave came to collect her, he let out a wolf-whistle.

'Hey, Lydia, you look so good. So beautiful! You will be the Belle of the Ball tonight – no doubt about that.'

His words touched her heart – she knew he meant them.